MW01279887

A Time For Justice
and
Other Frontier Tales

BY
KENT KAMRON

A TIME FOR JUSTICE
AND OTHER FRONTIER TALES

Author - Kent Kamron
Publisher - McCleery & Sons Publishing
Editor in Chief - Steve Tweed
Cover Design/Graphics - Robert Washnieski and Steve Hoffman

International Standard Book Number 0-9700624-1-9
Printed in the United States of America

INTRODUCTION

Kamron rides again, out of the mists from Northfield to Mingusville, writing with the swift fury of a surprise attack from Mosby's Raiders.

Having established firm roots among readers of historical fiction with his first book, *Charlie's Gold and Other Frontier Tales,* Kent Kamron returns with an even more compelling collection of suspenseful short stories. A *Time for Justice* takes off where the first volume left off, satisfying the reader's hunger for more tales of the wide prairie.

As publishers, we were intrigued to find that not all Kamron fans turned out to be devotees of the Wild West. Many reviewers of *Charlie's Gold* –men and women alike– said they loved the trick endings and plot lines, or the simplicity of the story telling, but admitted that *Charlie's Gold* was the first "western" book they had ever read. The host of North Dakota's highest rated radio talk show told his audience that he had devoured Charlie's Gold twice - and had read several stories aloud to his wife on a lonely stretch of highway. His comments made sense to the many who have attended readings by the author; Kamron's stories are so tightly written and dramatic, so fast paced and full of historical interest, that they make great listening too.

A *Time for Justice* puts you in the saddle, to wander the buttes and draws, the rivers and foothills of untamed territory, all the while on the lookout for trouble. A hammer cocks back in the dead of night, a weathered boot snaps a tinder branch...and I am reminded of the best work of Ernest Haycox, who wrote of unforgettable killers and cowards. And when Kamron hits his truest note, I was nostalgic for that classic storyteller of western lore, the towering Frederick Manfred.

Kent Kamron, the pen name of Del Dvoracek, is a Fargo, North Dakota writer who has published plays, short stories and magazine articles over the past several years. A *Time for Justice* is his second collection of highly praised short stories published under the name of McCleery and Sons.

Steve Tweed
Editorial Director
McCleery & Sons Publishing

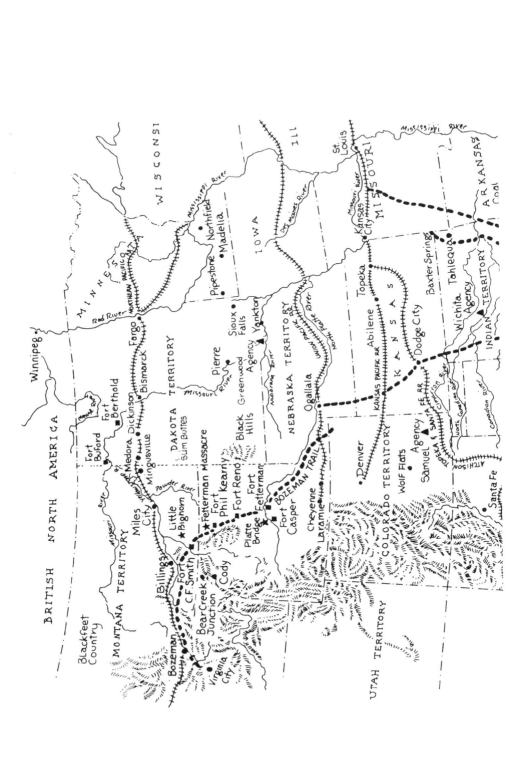

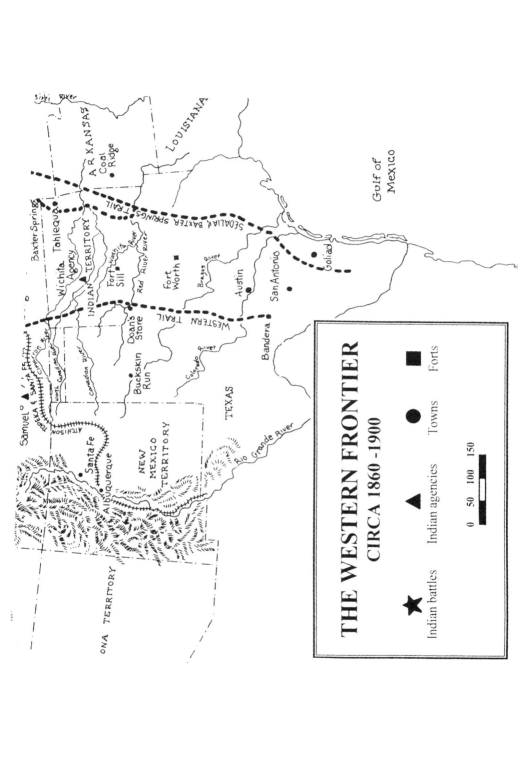

THE WESTERN FRONTIER
CIRCA 1860 -1900

★ Indian battles   ▲ Indian agencies   ● Towns   ■ Forts

0   50   100   150

Gulf of Mexico

LOUISIANA

ARKANSAS
Coal Ridge ●

Baxter Springs ●
Wichita ●
Tahlequah ●
Agency ▲
INDIAN TERRITORY

SEDALIA& BAXTER SPRINGS TRAIL

Fort Worth ■
Fort Sill ■
Red River
Washita River
Brazos River
Austin ●
San Antonio ●
Goliad ●

WESTERN TRAIL

Bandera ●
Doan's Store ●
Buckskin Run ●

Colorado River

TEXAS

Samuel ▲
TOPEKA & SANTA FE
ATCHISON
Cimarron River
North Canadian River
Canadian River

Santa Fe ●
Albuquerque ●

NEW MEXICO TERRITORY

Rio Grande River

ONA TERRITORY

Mippi River

TABLE OF CONTENTS

ABOUT THE ILLUSTRATOR

Robert Washnieski has achieved success as one of the Upper Midwest's most sought-after and praised fine art illustrators. His three decade long award-winning career has encompassed corporate and private commissioned works and high profile illustrations in countless periodicals. Washnieski and his family live in Fargo, North Dakota. His talents may be seen by visiting www.mpcentral.com/washnieski.

Art is life. It is my pleasure to create ideas and build thoughts by honoring subjects of great diversity in both fine art and commercial art applications...expressing the moments of life and communicating those thoughts in moments of time.

Robert J. Washnieski

FROM THE AUTHOR

Getting this second collection of short western stories out kept me busy writing over the last year. Spinning yarns about the West keeps me going, and if you have as much fun reading these stories as I did writing them, you'll make me one happy cowpoke.

I like the fiction end of western writing, but a few of the stories in this book are based on actual happenings. Liane, a good friend of mine, turned me on to the story line for *The Reward*, which has a lot of truth in it. *Old Strike*, strikes close to home too, as you'll discover, and *Saturday in Mingusville* might bring a slight revelation.

Reading through my library and digging up material is half the battle in penning these tales, though that sort of research settles real easy with me. Since the last book, *Charlie's Gold and Other Frontier Tales*, I've made the rounds again visiting places which make for good settings in corners of the West many of us have forgotten about or don't know about. For the most part, these are stories your kids can read. You'll discover some occasional violence, but coming through the late 1800's in a lawless land made that sort of thing on the western frontier unavoidable.

Once again, I'd like to thank a few people who took a moment to read these tales and offer suggestions and revisions. These ruffians are Marty, Sharon, Ted, Tony and Merry. And I should add "Old Bill" to this list even though he mostly just reads. I also remain deeply indebted to Ver, my wife, who continues to stay up late at night while I try to entertain her with the first draft of each new story. She gets her two-cents in here and there, and you'll find an example of her two-cents when you get through the first tale.

And finally, my sincere appreciation goes to Steve, my editor, and to McCleery & Sons Publishing for their continued support.

Kent Kamron

Dedicated to my wife
and two sons

An Act of Kindness

They had been riding hard for three days over a rocky desert plain. Even though they were walking their horses for the better part of the last hour, the animals were lathered heavily, their heads hanging low. The two riders were just as weary, hot from the penetrating sun, their bodies wringing with sweat and packed with dirt.

"Orin, if we don't find water soon, we ain't going to make it."

Orin nodded, his throat so parched he didn't want to answer. "Don't know if this was such a good idea," said Everett.

Again Orin nodded. "You might be right, little brother."

There was three years difference in their ages, but side by side with their week old beards and heavy eyebrows, it would be hard to tell them apart from fifty feet away. Orin was just a bit shorter, Everett maybe fifteen pounds heavier. They both wore pistols with black grips in dark holsters, and their hats, though old and tattered, were bent and shaped the same way.

"Better give these boys a breather," said Everett as he stepped off his horse. They both loosed the cinches on their saddles and scouted the area ahead as they walked on the loose, desert sand.

Two hours slipped by, the sun showing about three o'clock in the sky. They heaved themselves back into the saddles and plodded along a line of low rocks. Inside of a few minutes, Orin spotted a homestead. "There Everett, look over there."

A mile or better away they could see a little shack, a corral nearby with a lone buckboard next to it. There was not one tree in sight.

"Looks like some sort of civilization," said Orin.

They let their horses pick their way over a small mound of rocks and headed off toward the setting. There appeared to be no one around, though a small, shoddy garden plot with some half-green tops spurting out of the ground indicated someone must be living here.

"If somebody's got a garden out in this miserable country," said Orin, "gotta be water near by."

As they neared, they could see a spring on the far side of the garden plot among some rocks, a small pool no more than five feet across, but it was water. They hurried their horses across the yard, past the shack, past a makeshift shelter straight for the waterhole.

Both horses and riders drank of the cool spring for the longest time. The brothers dropped their holsters, took off their shirts, hats and neckerchiefs and splashed the refreshing water up over themselves, giddy with excitement.

They were so busy splashing around that they did not notice the figure approach behind them until it was too late. They both slowly stood not to cause any alarm, especially since they were looking down the muzzle of a double-barrel shotgun.

She was about fifty, wearing a long dress, her hair done up in a bun. She held the gun steady like she knew how to use it, and her voice was strong and firm when she spoke. "You boys usually sneak up and take hospitality freely?"

Orin was careful with his answer. "Ma'am, we've been traveling long and hard with no water for the past two days. We regret that our desire for water seemed to outride our manners of hospitality, and for that we sincerely apologize."

She saw that the two men had dropped their weapons to the ground. From that gesture alone, she figured the two young men were probably just drifters.

"Don't suppose you've eaten in two days either?" she asked.

"No, ma'am," they both answered in unison.

She held the shotgun steady for a few seconds, then lowered it. "Soon's you boys are cleaned up, come up to the house. You can put your horses in the lean-to. Ain't much hay, but it's all I got for now."

"Yes, ma'am."

Orin and Everett soaked up some more of the water, got clean shirts out of their saddlebags, put their horses in the lean-to and unsaddled them.

They left their guns on a porch bench when they entered the house. It was not much of a house, siding shoved together with cracks here and there that let in light, and some homemade furniture. The meal was bread, smoked beef and coffee. They ate as much as they wanted and remarked how good the hot coffee tasted even though it was a hot day.

When they finished their meal, Everett offered his thanks. "We do appreciate your hospitality, but we'd best be going. We have some hard riding ahead of us."

Her face suddenly sagged, as if about to cry.

Orin couldn't help but notice the glum look. "Ma'am, you live out here all alone?"

Her face saddened even more, and then she broke out crying. The two boys sat down again, not at all sure how they should respond.

"My man left the better part of two days ago on his horse. We got cattle south of here. I'm sure something has happened to him. I searched two days on foot, but couldn't find him."

"You don't have another horse?"

"We did, but he got a snake bite on the nose a few weeks back. Poor thing swelled up, couldn't breath. Albert had to shoot him."

Orin and Everett stood at the same time. "Ma'am, you point us in the right direction and we'll try to find him."

"God bless you," she said.

By the time they were saddled up, she had given them some

directions where they might search. They were to follow the rock ridge for three miles where they would find a passage to a small valley. She cautioned them it was steep in a lot of places, but once they found the creek the cattle would more than likely be scattered about.

They loped their horses the entire distance, realizing they had only about four hours of daylight left. By the time they found the narrow creek, their idea of a thorough search seemed almost futile. The area was laden with jutting rocks, narrow passageways, steep on both sides. But the valley extended a few miles, and in the distance they could see some cattle.

It was still hot, the sun still beating severely for the time of day, but the two had their bellies full of food and drink and felt a new sense of vigor. Orin took the right side of the valley, Everett the left. They agreed they would head south as far as the light would take them, keeping each other in sight whenever they could. On occasion they would each fire one shot, to see if they could get a response from the man called Albert. His wife said he had a rifle and a pistol, which would be a way of signaling. If he were alive, they could expect a shot in return.

They set out moving as fast as they could, both taking the trails to each side of the valley. They were no more than a couple miles apart at all times, and on occasion they could hear each other's shots as they continued their search.

Two hours into the search, Everett fired his pistol and was about to put it away when he heard a rifle shot up ahead. He spurred his horse on through a steep set of rocks, and after riding another few minutes, he fired his pistol again.

Again a rifle shot came back, muffled a bit, but definitely a rifle shot.

Everett knew he found Albert. He rode up to a rise where he could see across the valley and fired three shots in a row. In less than a minute he saw Orin ride down a slope and head across the valley. In no time at all Orin had joined him, and now the two spread out as

Everett fired another shot.

The rifle report came back at them, and within a few minutes they found the man called Albert.

"Howdy, boys," he said. He was below them about fifteen feet on a rock shelf, sitting in the shade, and had a piece of wood on each side of one leg bound with a lariat. "Wouldn't happen to have a canteen with you, would you?"

"Sure would," said Everett as he carefully climbed down to the man. "You must be Albert."

"None other," he said as he gulped at the water. "I knew somebody would find me. Course I didn't know if'n it was going to be this week or next, or maybe next year."

At least the man had a sense of humor, Everett was thinking.

"Alma send you boys after me?"

"If Alma's your wife, yep. Where's your horse?"

"In a ravine about a mile and a half that way," he pointed. "Cleo and I fell down a hundred foot cliff. She was bad. Had to shoot her." He stared into the face of Everett. "Ain't that somethin'? Had the same two horses for nigh on to twelve years, and then I lose 'em both two weeks apart." He settled into a more comfortable position. "This is as far as I could crawl. Ain't no way out the other way."

Orin lowered a rope, and with Albert secured under the arm pits, the two managed to pull him up amid groans and grunts. They hoisted him into the saddle on one horse, and the two brothers rode double on the other.

Just about sundown they returned to Albert's home place. His wife was in tears as she hugged her man, helped get him inside to a cot. By the time Orin and Everett had unsaddled their horses and returned to the house, Albert had a couple glasses on the table and a bottle of whiskey. It was obviously a home brew, not as smooth as the whiskey the brothers were used to, but it was the best hospitality the couple could offer.

"We'll be off at sunup," said Everett. "Got a long ride ahead of us. We'll sleep in the lean-to, if it's all right with you."

"You'll have breakfast before you leave, won't you?" Albert's wife asked.

They looked at each other. "We couldn't turn that down, ma'am."

They excused themselves and in short time had opened their saddle rolls and dozed off tired as could be.

The desert night was cool, but the sun coming up in the morning had a sudden waking effect. Orin was the first to stir. He crawled out from under his blanket and slipped his boots on. He stood and stretched for the longest time, strapped his gunbelt on and headed for the water hole.

He had gone no more than a few feet when he heard a heavy voice shout, "Hold it right there and put your hands up!"

Orin saw the shadowy figures ahead, six men partially hidden behind rocks, their rifles pointed at him.

"Everett!" he shouted to wake him up.

Everett rolled out of his blanket with his pistol in hand. As soon as the men saw the weapon, they cut loose with their rifles bringing down the two brothers without either having a chance to return a shot.

Albert's wife rushed out of the house when she heard the gunfire. She approached the two downed youngsters, stared at their blood smeared shirts. Moments later, Albert hobbled out and stood alongside his wife, hardly able to believe what he was seeing.

The Deputy tipped his hat. "Albert, Alma. These two are the Dutcher brothers. They robbed the bank at Buckskin Run."

"My God," gasped Alma. "Did you have to kill them? They was such nice boys!"

The Deputy grunted. "They didn't give Zeke and Jordan a chance.

"They killed Zeke and Jordie?" asked Albert.

Alma couldn't believe her eyes. "Albert, they could have got away, but they offered to find you. They was such kind boys."

In the distance they could hear hoof beats as three riders came on at an easy lope.

"That's the Sheriff", said the Deputy. "We split up yesterday morning."

Sheriff Dutton rode up and stopped, stared at the two dead men on the ground.

"What happened here, Emil?" he asked as he got off his horse.

"We got the Dutcher brothers. Trailed em' right up to Albert's place, surprised em' this morning."

The Sheriff glared at the Deputy. "Emil, for crissake! These ain't the Dutchers! We caught the Dutchers yesterday afternoon!"

The Sheriff stared into the faces of the six posse members. "Did you ask them to identify themselves?"

None of the men spoke.

"Well, did you?"

No one spoke.

Albert put an arm around his wife and hobbled along with her back to the house. The posse members, all glum faced, looked down at the two slain men. They were silent for a moment, and then their ears were filled with the wailing screams of Albert's wife.

Author's note: *Such unfortunate events sometimes happened in the West, and for those who feel the story was too brutal, perhaps you will find this alternate ending much more to your satisfaction.*

"You'll have breakfast before you leave, won't you?" Albert's wife asked.

The two brothers looked at each other. "We couldn't turn that down."

They excused themselves and in short time had opened their saddle rolls and dozed off, tired as could be.

The desert night was cool, but the sun coming up in the morning had a sudden waking effect. Orin was the first to stir. He crawled out from under his blanket and slipped his boots on. He stretched for the longest time, then headed for the water hole. Everett followed a short time later.

The two brothers had a quick breakfast, thanked the couple for their kindness and rode off.

Later that day, Sheriff Dutton and a twelve man posse rode in, the men bedraggled, their horses much the same. While the men watered their horses and filled their canteens, the Sheriff questioned Albert and Alma.

"Couple men robbed the Buckskin Run bank a few days back," he said.

"You don't say," said Albert. "Did they get any money?"

"About seventy dollars was all. They wasn't very good robbers. Missed the big cash box completely."

"Kill anyone?"

"No, but scared the hell out of everybody. Zeke and Jordan think it was the Dutcher brothers from Viper Springs. Seen anybody ride through here lately?"

Albert was silent, looked at his wife. "Nope."

"What happened to your leg, Albert?"

"Broke it a few days back. But I think I got it set good."

"Where's your horses?"

Albert flashed his eyes at Alma. "Had to shoot old Brutus, and Cleo run off a few days back."

Sheriff Dutton stared at Albert, looked critically at Alma. "Well, I think we'll head back to town. We've been in the saddle four straight days. Besides, seventy dollars ain't much to chase after, and we ain't fer certain it was the Dutchers anyway. Want me to send Doc out here?"

"Wouldn't hurt. And have Charlie send me out a couple saddle horses. I'll pay him next time I see him."

"Right. Bye Alma."

When the posse was gone, Alma gave Albert a stern look. "Albert, you lied to them."

"Well, ain't my life worth at least seventy bucks?" he said as he gave her a big hug. And then he added, "Get out the cards, Alma. It's gonna be at least a week a'for the Doc gets here."

Silent Revenge

Molly was only nine when they found her. Pete and Inge Tollefson with their four children were driving in to Newton for supplies and simply stopped along the way at the Garret farm to be neighborly.

What they discovered on that balmy, October day was Molly's mother and father dead in the yard. Her father had been shot in the chest, his body lying under the fence by the corral. Her mother was lying face down in the dirt between the corral and the home place. Next to her was a double barrel shotgun.

Molly was sitting on the ground between the two, seemingly all right, wearing a nightshirt that was neither dirty nor torn. She sat in silence, her gaze nothing more than a glaring stare, and although Mrs. Tollefson spoke to her, she could not answer.

The petrified look on her face bore the truth of the tragedy that had transpired on the Garret farm, but she could not speak, could not even respond to the most simple of questions.

Pete Tollefson entered the farm home and discovered everything in order. The only thing out of the ordinary was that the corral gate, which held in Garret's five horses, was open, and the horses were gone.

The Tollefsons left the bodies where they lay, careful not to disturb anything. They wrapped Molly in a blanket, placed her in between the two of them on the wagon seat and drove into Newton.

Later that day, Sheriff Gordon Stillwell, Doc Folsom and Pete Tollefson returned to the Garret place where the Sheriff carried out an investigation.

On examining Garret's body, they discovered a cut across his face. The Doc said since blood had dripped freely from the wound, it was very probable Garret had suffered the facial cut before he was shot. Both barrels of the shotgun lying next to Mrs. Garret had been discharged, indicating she must have fired the weapon before she was killed.

They loaded up the two bodies in the back of the wagon and were about to head back to town when Garret's horses came running across the plain. They ran into the corral just like someone had herded them and stood near the small lean-to, as if waiting for some hay to be tossed at them.

"Only four came back," said Pete. "His big black saddle horse is missing."

Pete went through the lean-to checking out the saddles that Garret owned. "One of his saddles is missing, too."

The three men pieced together the scenario as best they could. It appeared sometime near dawn, someone had entered Garret's corral with the intention of stealing a horse. Since Molly was still in her nightshirt, the intrusion probably took place before the Garrets had even prepared breakfast.

Because of the consistency of the clotted blood found on both bodies, Doc Folsom was reasonably sure the killings did not take place the night before.

Sheriff Stillwell put it best. "My guess is Garret came outside without a weapon to see what was up with his horses. He tried to stop the thief and got killed in the process."

Both the Doc and Pete Tollefson agreed that was quite possible.

"Then Mrs. Garret came out, fired both barrels and was killed right afterward."

They also agreed to that.

"And after he kilt them, he stole Garret's best saddle horse," said Pete.

The Sheriff nodded. That seemed like the best scenario. He looked at the shotgun lying next to Mrs. Garret's body. "I wonder if she hit him."

"She was a good shot with a rifle," said Pete. "Pretty good chance if she got off both barrels, she did some damage."

The Sheriff estimated the distance from the corral to where Mrs. Garret's body lay at about twenty-five yards. Buckshot at that range could raise a lot of welts on a man's body.

That was their best guess at what had happened on that day at the Garret farm. That was exactly the order of events, and the only person who knew for certain was little Molly, but of course she could not speak since that day or any day after.

Molly was adopted by Doc Folsom and his wife, who had no children, and she took their name. Four years after the incident, in 1873, the Folsoms moved to Topeka where the Doc decided to retire. The Folsoms had, over the years, given Molly every opportunity for an education, and though she could not speak, she could hear perfectly. She learned to read and write and had developed an unusual skill for facts and figures. She was smart and charming in her silent manner, and she was well liked.

While in Topeka, Doc Folsom became acquainted with Fred Harvey, an Englishman who at the age of fifteen had immigrated to America. Mr. Harvey had worked for the Kansas Pacific for some time, and because the food was so bad at the various stops along the line, he decided to open a restaurant at the Topeka depot.

He served excellent food and had gained a solid reputation for service and quality. Doc Folsom frequented the Harvey Restaurant quite often, and it was through him that the Doc found a position for his adopted daughter, Molly.

At the age of eighteen, she went to work for Fred Harvey as a kitchen helper, but in short time he recognized her skills, and soon she was in a management position handling the financial affairs of his business. The pen and paper was her mainstay, and she was successful from the onset.

As Fred Harvey opened additional depot restaurants along the Santa Fe Railroad line, Molly Folsom traveled along to each establishment to set the books in order.

In 1880 Molly found herself working in Santa Fe, New Mexico, the farthest reach of the railroad at the time. She was twenty years old, and although she was very attractive, she did not have any suitors simply because she could not speak. The waitresses, known as the *Harvey Girls* up and down the line, always attracted suitors. Too many of them found husbands here in the west where young ladies were scarce, so Mr. Harvey wrote into their contracts, that if they married before the end of their first year of employment, they must forfeit half of their wages.

That deterred some from marriage, but most waitresses, after the year was up, married and moved on. Unfortunately, such was not the case for Molly Folsom, and many nights as she whiled away the hours reading in her room, tears interrupted her unwanted solitude. Daily, the death of her mother and father plagued her beyond any understanding. As much as she wanted to, she was unable to share such disturbing thoughts with anyone else. Her days kept her busy, but her nights were filled with depression without any hope, it seemed, of erasing that tragic day so many years ago.

She had become private over the last few years, but had continued to write in her diary, which was her only consolation, a means to verbalize on paper what she could not verbalize in public. She had become a recluse she knew, yet she possessed a determined strength to maintain a professional manner in her daily dealings. She had gained some friends, but whenever a group of them were together, she could rarely contribute to the topic of conversation, only respond with an occasional raising of an eyebrow, or with a frown, or with a smile, or with a laugh without sound. Once in a while, she would write a note.

There were many nights when she simply cried the night away in her room, but such occasions she never shared with anyone.

One morning when she was busy with the books in the lobby

of the depot restaurant, a throng of people who had arrived on the train entered and made their way into the dining room. The Harvey Girls were prepared, seated all the passengers and had their meals served in short time.

It was not Molly's position to enter in with the business of the servants, but she happened to be tallying some figures when a man, some ten feet away, was paying his bill. Molly stared incredulously at him, observed the many scarred spots on the side of his face and neck. In an instant her memory returned to the farm north of Newton. She could visualize this man vividly in her memory, saw her mother fire the shotgun, saw the pellets strike the man in the face as he attempted to ride away on her father's horse. Then the horror as the man aimed his pistol and killed her with a bullet through the head.

The memory was so real, so close to Molly that she shuddered and sighed a grunt, the first audible sound she had made in some twelve years. She wanted to scream out, summon someone to come to her aide, to prevent this man from getting back on the train, but she had no recourse. No one would understand her, no one knew he was the man who murdered her parents.

As he passed by no more than feet away, he gave her a passing glance, but he did not recognize her after twelve years.

The man walked out of the depot onto the railroad platform and stood for a few seconds. Molly was frantic. There must be some way she could stop him from getting back on the train, but she could not function, could not remotely think how she could detain him.

Other passengers now moved freely onto the platform when the whistle blew, the first signal that everyone should board. The man moved along with the crowd toward the train. She could only see the black, western cut hat as the crowd merged toward the boarding steps.

The whistle blew three shrill bursts. Steam shot out from the sides of the engine engulfing the platform in a sea of mist.

"Board!" she heard the conductor shout, and in seconds the

train chugged off, the steam obliterating its view. Molly sank into a lounge chair, pressed her hand to her breast and sobbed, the first real sobs she had heard in most of her lifetime.

When the train had left the station, she slowly rose from the chair, her eyes filled with tears. She looked out onto the empty platform, her heart sinking.

And then she saw it. The black hat! Across the tracks and walking toward the city was the man in the black hat. He was not a passenger on the train!

She hurriedly grabbed her shawl and wrapped it about her, then briskly started along the street in the direction the man was headed. She had walked no more than five minutes when she saw the man enter the Santa Fe Hotel.

He might well have either a temporary or a permanent room, which one she did not know. But she dare not enter, dare not pursue the man any further. She returned to the depot restaurant and spent the rest of the day unable to function in any reasonable capacity.

That night, her nerves on end, she retired to her room at the dormitory adjacent to the depot. She opened her diary and was about to write her discovery, but then hesitated. She made notes about her day, but refused making any reference to the man who killed her parents. The mere idea of penning this man into her private thoughts was abhorrent and foul.

For the next few days she was alert. The man had returned for evening meals and always wore the same buckskin jacket with frills, tan canvas pants and stovetop black boots.

He became a frequent visitor, arriving almost daily at the same time for his evening meal, and by careful listening, she managed to pick up small bits of information. His name was Aaron Kingsley, a former railroad worker. He did not have an occupation at the moment, but was residing at the Santa Fe Hotel on a weekly basis. One day she saw him ride by on a bay horse and feared perhaps he was leaving town. Her heart jumped a beat, but later in the day he returned.

Rumor had it he was a land speculator, but no one knew which company he worked for, or whether his interests were private.

During the next few days, Molly gleaned every piece of information she could gather on him. While dining with some rough looking characters, he had been overheard talking about the "poor quality of the whores" at the downtown Heart Saloon and Dance Parlor.

On another occasion, the man known as Kingsley had arrived at the depot restaurant with his face beaten up considerably. While at the table, Sheriff Ulven called on him and asked a few questions. Evidently the man had been involved in a saloon brawl the night before where several shots had been fired. Kingsley was now wearing a pistol, something she had not noticed before. Her worst fear was the man would be thrown out of the city, but the next day he was back.

Evidently the man always had money to spend on women and whiskey, and if trouble was brewing, it seemed he was always involved.

One evening when Kingsley had finished his meal, he entered the lobby where Molly was working. He had seen her before, and she had made eye contact with him, but this night he was definitely paying more attention to her. She saw his interest and she did not pretend to be uninterested.

"You're a purdy lady," he said unexpectedly. "I understand you don't talk."

She nodded, keeping her eyes on him.

He looked around the lobby to make sure nobody else was present. "I imagine your affliction must hold you back some from having a good time."

She nodded again.

He licked his lips, glanced about once again. "Maybe some night you and me could have a good time." He pressed a heavy smile into his face, waiting for a response.

She nodded again.

"I know'd," he said. "I been lookin' at you the past few weeks. Don't matter none you can't talk. Know what I mean?"

She forced a smile, nodded again. She drew a figure on a piece of paper, the configuration of the dormitory in which she was staying. He recognized the building next door. She drew the location of her room, the first along a corridor inside the dormitory.

A look of envy crossed his face.

She penciled in *midnight* next to the room.

"Tonight?" he asked.

She nodded.

"Any trouble getting in the front door?"

She shook her head, reached into her pocket and showed him the key.

He smiled and raised his eyebrows. "Midnight. I'll be there." He left the lobby and disappeared into the night.

Just short of midnight, Aaron Kingsley made his way in the shadows to the dormitory, and was not at all surprised the front door was left unlocked. He was in a reception room, dimly lit by the moonlight of two windows. He allowed his eyes to adjust, then silently crossed to the hallway. When he entered her room, once again the moonlight pouring through a window gave the only light. She was sitting on her bed, her face and body a dark silhouette against the outside light. She was clad in her nightgown and beckoned him.

Kingsley smiled, removed his buckskin jacket and pistol belt, then pulled off his boots. She could smell the liquor on his breath when he sat on the edge of her bed, felt her nerves crawl as he slowly unbuttoned his shirt.

At that moment she slid back a bit and let the moonlight shine on a piece of paper on her lap. She handed him the sheet, and though he was puzzled he held it up to catch more light coming through the window. On the paper she had drawn rough figures of a man lying on the ground and a woman pointing a shotgun at a man on a horse.

Kingsley's eyes widened as he stared at the drawing, and when he looked up she was pointing a derringer at him. In the dim light she saw the fear creep into his face as he made the connection.

That's all she wanted.

He gaped as the first bullet ripped into him, the slug hitting him in the chest. She fired the second round, which struck him directly in the heart. He slumped forward, the blood from his chest oozing all over her nightgown and bed sheets.

She opened her mouth, and with the force of twelve years of silence she screamed so loud it even startled her.

She screamed again and again until the door to her room banged open. Several of the dorm girls entered, their lamps glowing, revealing the dead man on the bed, the blood stains on Molly's nightgown.

"My god!" someone shouted. "Get the sheriff!"

A half-hour later Sheriff Ulven arrived with a handful of men. There was no question in his mind what had transpired in Molly's room. He was ever so polite, and apologized for the insolent behavior of the man named Kingsley.

"He was bad all around, Miss Molly," he told her. "He deserved what he got, and there ain't no court of law going to hold you accountable for this."

The newspaper labeled the killing as self-defense against Kingsley, and made it clear the man had made an attempt to violate her. The news that Molly Folsom had regained her speech received equal prominence in the same issue.

No one ever suspected Molly had set the man up, and since no one ever questioned her background, the ordeal that had plagued her for so many years never came to light.

A short time after the incident, a rancher traveling by rail happened by the Santa Fe depot. He caught the charms of Miss Molly and had some charm of his own, and within two months of their first meeting, they were married. Miss Molly Folsom, like so many of the Harvey Girls, finally bid farewell to the life of the Harvey Restaurant. She moved on west and never returned.

A Time For Justice

Deputy Len Bradmiller stood at the corner of the Buckskin Hotel, his lanky frame leaning against a post as he rolled a cigarette. He no sooner got it lit when three riders came around the corner and trotted past him on the street. The three stopped in front of the Green Bull Saloon, tied up their horses and went inside.

Len threw down his cigarette and hurried to the Sheriff's office.

"Bill," he said to the Sheriff when he entered. "They're back, all three of 'em."

Sheriff Bill Long stood up and strapped his gunbelt on. "You sure it's them?"

"Yep. It's Rube Calloway all right. He's got that sawed off double barrel, and the Hengsley brothers are with him. Ain't hard to recognize that batch of scum."

Sheriff Bill Long did not have the appearance of the average sheriff. He was a foot shorter than Len and carried fifty extra pounds around his girth. Every day he wore a blue shirt, and canvas pants held up by suspenders. If he were to wear a suit, one would easily mistake him for a fat banker. For the past eight years, Bill Long had done a pretty good job as sheriff of Buckskin Run.

His rules were simple. Drunks got a day to sober up. Those who were fighting got a week and a fine. Those drinking and fighting got a week and a bigger fine. Almost everyone the Sheriff put in jail was a drinker and a fighter. Once they sobered up, they had to pay a fine to get out of jail or spend another week, so most paid their fine, which paid for most of the Sheriff's salary.

Those few rules fit most of the problems in town, but they didn't fit Rube and his two cutthroat buddies.

"See if you can find Mayor Ingells and get him over to the saloon," the Sheriff said.

"Don't start nothin' till I get there," said Len.

"I won't." As if Len could help. The Sheriff knew Len couldn't hit a barn with his six-shooter even if he was standing inside. But he was good company and liked by everyone in town. Better yet, he was part-time, which the town could afford.

The piano at the Green Bull Saloon was lively and loud, an indication that most of the outlying cowboys were already carousing. A dozen horses or more were already at the hitching post outside, and just as many at the Buford Inn across the street. The town was gearing up for a normal Saturday night, except tonight the Sheriff had Rube Calloway to contend with.

When the Sheriff entered the saloon, he spotted the threesome right away. They stood at the bar with drinks in their hands, looking over the crowd. The Sheriff knew their purpose; they were searching out another victim. A month ago when the three made an appearance in Buckskin Run, Charlie Hicks ended up dead in an alley, shot in the back with a load of buckshot. Naturally, the eight hundred or so dollars he had won at poker that night was gone.

Six weeks before that, a similar thing happened to young Henry Kranz. Some said Henry had barely a hundred dollars on him, not big money, but enough to kill for. Judge Fuhrman, Mayor Ingells, the Sheriff and his Deputy all knew Rube Calloway and his cronies had murdered them. The only time Rube Calloway showed up with his two buddies, Pate and Drury, was when they ran short of money. Favorville, some twenty-five miles to the south, complained of the same problem, as did Summer Springs, forty miles west. These boys could smell out money like termites smell out a wagon of timber.

They were killers all right, but no one could prove it. Frontier justice required a witness to the shootings or some real strong evidence, but no one saw the murders take place. After each killing, Rube Calloway had the audacity to stick around town a few days afterward, spending money like he was some rich rancher. Killing a man was bad enough, but to hang around after the killing, acting so pious and using up the victim's money was too much for the Sheriff.

Kirk at the piano was at his best tonight, thumping loud and fierce with his big fingers, blowing out a puff of cigar smoke every eight beats. A couple girls leaned on the piano showing off their wares and waiting for some cowboys to buy them some watered down drinks. They weren't having much luck since there didn't seem to be any takers at the moment, but it was early.

Cards were flying at the tables. The rattling of chips was a nice sound for the winners but a bad one for the losers.

Sheriff Bill Long slowly walked past the three men, eyed the pistols and rifles of the two with Rube. Rube carried a .45 tucked into his belt and had his sawed off shotgun lying on the bar.

"Well, now, if it ain't Sheriff Bill, the law of Buckskin Run," said Rube as the Sheriff stepped up. Rube spit some brown juice at a spittoon. He scowled and dipped a set of bushy eyebrows when he missed. He was full bearded, not a big man, but sturdy and stocky, easily able to carry two one-hundred-pound sacks a mile. His two cronies were built pretty much the same, both with full beards. They all wore clothes that were long in need of washing. In fact, the Sheriff could smell the scummy odor coming off of them.

"H'lo Rube," said the Sheriff. "You boys in town for a little fun, are ya?"

"Might say that."

"Maybe pick up a little cash at the tables?"

"Maybe," said Rube. "How's the sheriffing business?"

Bill Long pulled a face. "Oh, been pretty quiet since we instigated the new town rule."

"And what rule might that be?"

The Sheriff pointed to the wall behind Rube. "Gotta give up

yer hardware when you're in a saloon. Rifles and shotguns behind the bar, pistols on the wall."

Rube, Pate and Drury eyed the gunbelts lining the wall, then looked over the crowd. Almost everyone was looking back. The card shuffling and chip stacking came to an abrupt halt when Kirk stopped playing the piano.

"Course we're only staying fer a few hours," said Rube. "No need to hang up our…"

"All guns," the Sheriff interrupted.

Rube scowled and spit out another gob of brown goo, half of which hung on his beard. "Well, now, Mister Lawman, sposin' we don't care to give up our guns?"

The swinging door to the bar squeaked open and Deputy Len Bradmiller and the Mayor walked in. Len was carrying a shotgun, which caught Rube's attention.

"I see you got the Deputy and the Mayor as back up," said Rube. "Ain't that convenient." He looked directly at Len and laughed. "Hope you got enough weight to hold that shotgun down, Mr. Deputy, cause if'n it goes off, it's liable to kick you right out the door."

Several of the men at the tables chuckled at the comment.

"Maybe it will," retorted Len. "But not till I fill you full of holes."

Rube Calloway straightened up. "Now that ain't no way to talk to somebody who's hankerin' to comply with the rules of the town." Rube turned to his friends. "Pate, Drury, we sure 'nuf want to comply with the rules of the town, don't we?"

Pate and Drury put their rifles on the bar, and all three gave up their pistols.

"Thanks, boys," said the Sheriff. "You can pick them up when you leave."

In seconds the bar was back to normal. Kirk was thumping out a lively tune and the girls started charming the cowboys once again. In every corner, gamblers made their bets, shouting and laughing, and in general everyone was back to having a good time.

Bill, Len and Mayor Ingells grabbed a corner table and ordered some beers. The Sheriff kept his eye on Rube and his two cronies.

In short time, the three ambled over to a faro table and placed a few bets, and after losing a few rounds, they settled at a table with some of the local town boys. Soon they were all playing poker.

"Len," said the Sheriff. "When we leave, you go over to the Buford Inn and tell Huey to keep an eye out on the big winners. Then go find Burl and see if he'll do some snoopin' for us." Burl Campbell ran the general store, and was a close friend of the Sheriff's. "If any of these three killers show up at Buford's, I want Burl to let me know immediately."

The Sheriff looked over at the bartender. "I'll get Emery to do the same over here." He turned to Mayor Ingells. "Fred, you get somebody to stand watch with you outside somewhere in the shadows. These boys head out of town for any reason, you get hold of me."

The Mayor was looking at the three and was fidgety. "You think these boys will kill somebody tonight?"

"Hope not," said the Sheriff. "Only way we can prevent it is keep an eye on 'em. It'd be too obvious if Len or me stuck around. We got to play into their hands. When we leave, they'll loosen up a bit."

The Mayor was sweating. "I don't know about standing around outside. Somebody might get killed."

The Sheriff scoffed at the Mayor. "What the hell you want to do, go home to bed? You and the town committee told us to do something about these three scum suckin' killers, now dammit, don't go sour on us."

"Sorry," the Mayor apologized. "Guns ain't my kind of livin', and I hate to see somebody get killed for nothin'."

"We don't want no killin' either," said Len, backing up the Sheriff.

The Mayor removed his hat and wiped the sweat off his forehead with a handkerchief.

"Fred," said the Sheriff. "You walk out of here like you're goin' home. Tell Emery goodnight as you leave, and don't even glance over at those three killers."

"Right." He stood up and walked past the bartender and went straight out the door without saying a word.

"Finish your beer, Len. You're next."

Len finished his beer and left. When he was gone, a few of the Sheriff's friends sat down at his table. He spent some time chatting with them, and a half-hour later he got up to leave.

Rube Calloway had his eyes on the Sheriff from the moment he stood up, and never took his eyes off him until he was out the door.

Bill Long went directly to his office, where he sat reading a newspaper for the first part of the night, then busied himself with some paperwork to pass away the time. Len showed up occasionally, keeping Bill informed on the night's activities. So far, the three men had remained in the Green Bull Saloon. Len reported that Jeskin and Tabbert from the Bar-T ranch were winning at the tables. Three more riders from the Bar-T rode in with Jeskin and Tabbert, and it was a good bet the same five would ride together back to the ranch later on. All five of the cowboys carried six-shooters, so neither the Sheriff nor the Deputy was too concerned about their safety. At the Buford, old Barry Krupp, a down and out prospector, had stacked up a goodly amount of chips.

Pate and Drury Hengsley had showed up at the Buford for about a half-hour and then returned to the Green Bull. No one worried about Barry since he was rooming at the Keppler Hotel next door. The chance of him being targeted by the three was practically negligible.

At almost one in the morning, Len was pouring another cup of coffee with the Sheriff when the Mayor rushed in the door.

"They're gone! Rube and his buddies headed north toward Basin Creek!"

"Were they following somebody?" asked the Sheriff.

"How the hell do I know. There's fellas coming and going all the time."

"Are the Bar-T boys still at the saloon?"

"No, they were just leaving when I come over."

"All five together?"

"Yep."

The Sheriff stood, looked at his Deputy. "The Bar-T boys gotta cross Basin Creek. You don't suppose Rube and his scum are fool hardy enough to take on those five young cowpokes?"

Len smirked. "Well, if they lie in wait, they could pick off three at once, then work on the remaining two. There's a bright enough moon tonight to get a clear shot."

"Dammit!" said Bill. "Let's go!"

He and his Deputy ran out the back of the jail where their horses were saddled. They mounted and headed north out of town.

The moon was almost full, and not a cloud in the sky. They pressed their horses following the dirt path that led to the creek. For fifteen minutes they kept their animals in a steady lope, and when they reached Basin Creek they ran through the water without slowing. In another few minutes they saw some horses ahead, all stopped on the road. As they neared, they could tell that two of the men were on the ground. Sheriff Bill Long feared the worst as they reined in.

"What happened? Who got shot?" asked the Sheriff as he jumped off his horse.

"That you, Bill?" asked one of the ranch hands.

"Who got shot?"

"Nobody," said young Tell Jeskins. "Sonny just stopped to puke."

"What the hell?" asked another. "Is it against the law to puke?"

All of the Bar-T boys were laughing now, even Sonny.

Bill could see the boys were no more than a mile away from their ranch house. "No," he said as he mounted his horse. "It ain't against the law to puke."

"What you doin' out here this time of night, Sheriff?" asked Tell.

"Looking for Rube Calloway and his two buddies."

"They shoot somebody?"

"I hope not. Come on, Len. Let's go back."

When the two reached the outskirts of town, they could see a small crowd of people congregated in front of the jail. Mayor Fred Ingells and Burl Campbell were among them.

"Now, what the hell?" said the Sheriff as he and Len dismounted. A half dozen men were standing around a buckboard, and in the box of the wagon lay someone covered with a tarp. Burl Campbell pulled the tarp back.

"Barry Krupp!" said the Deputy.

"Oh, lord," said the Sheriff.

Keppler from the hotel was in the crowd. "Old Barry came in about one o'clock, said he done good at the tables. He went to his room for a bit, and then said he was headed for the Green Bull. That's the last I seen of him."

"Where did you find him?"

Burl Campbell answered. "Couple of us heard the shot. Found him about a hundred yards back of the jail."

"My god, right in my own back yard." The Sheriff stared down at the old timer, his face as glum as could be. There were at least five bloody holes in his shirtfront, made by a scattergun, he was sure. Barry had spent a lifetime searching for gold and never found a nugget worth more than five dollars. Tonight he probably had the most money on him he had ever possessed.

"Shall I take him over to Jake's parlor?" Burl asked. Jake Obert was the town mortician.

"No," said the Sheriff. "Take him to the Doc's office. I'll ride with you. Fred, Len, you two come along."

They woke Doc Grove up and hauled Barry Krupp's body into his back office. Bill, Len, Burl Campbell and the Mayor all sat quietly while the Doc dug out the shots one by one.

"Number six," said the Doc as he dropped the final piece of buckshot in a metal tray. "Krupp took six pieces of buckshot from fairly close, I'd say. Big ones, too."

Burl Campbell examined the shot. He knew shot size well since he sold shells in his store. "Yep, big buckshot. 'Bout twelve to a shell and Barry took half of them."

Mayor Ingells shook his head. "And there ain't no way we can prove they done it."

"Nobody seen 'em get shot," said Burl.

Len folded his hands and slumped in his chair. "They got away with it again."

"No, maybe not" said Bill. He looked into the faces of the men. "There's no doubt in our minds, Rube, Pate and Drury killed old Barry, ain't that right?

They nodded in agreement.

"A month ago they killed Charlie Hicks. Before that it was Henry Kranz, and who knows how many others they done in. Let's not only think about the men they killed, but the wives and kids and other family and friends that suffered because of these murdering skunks."

Bill Long was silent for a few moments. "You fellas want to put these killers away for good?"

They nodded again.

"Then, let's do it."

The five men talked long into the night, and by the time they left the Doc's office, the sun had been up for a half-hour.

Just like Sheriff Bill Long figured, the three men showed up the next day about noon and came into the Green Bull Saloon where he was waiting for them. With the Sheriff were Len and four other men, all wearing stars on their shirts.

The arrest was quick and without incident. When the Sheriff marched them to the jail, they all laughed, bragging they would be out in a few days. There was no way anyone could hold them, they claimed.

"You ain't got no witnesses and you ain't got no proof," said Rube as the three were locked up.

Even Judge Fuhrman was reluctant to hold them under the circumstances, but the Sheriff was adamant and stood fast that he had proof to put them away for good, so the Judge went along with it.

A lawyer from Favorville was appointed as defense attorney for the three. He was usually drunk, but he was the only lawyer around for a hundred miles. The lawyer collected all the facts he needed in less than a day, and spent the rest of his time frequenting the local saloons. He maintained there was no way the murder of Barry Krupp could be pinned on the three, since every other person in town owned a shotgun, and there were no witnesses. So the three had no problem with him representing them.

A jury was easily assembled and the trial began a week after the three had been arrested. Men and women from twenty miles around filled every seat in the courthouse. Trials over cattle rustling and horse thieving occurred once in a while, but the excitement of a real murder trial was what drew the crowd.

The lawyer for the defense, weaving on his feet, began by calling up Rube, Pate and Drury one at a time. He only asked them two questions: where were they when the murder took place, and did they have any witnesses to substantiate their whereabouts at the time. Of course, all three vouched for each other, stating they had spent the night at their camp five miles west of town. An earlier investigation showed they had indeed camped on the spot they indicated.

As they lied their way through the questions, their faces burned with smirks of contempt.

When it was Sheriff Bill Long's turn to question the men, he asked Pate and Drury if they had been with Rube Calloway the night of the murder, to which they both said they had.

"According to Doc Grove, Barry Krupp was killed at close range with a shotgun," the Sheriff stated. "Was it possible someone stole Rube Calloway's shotgun the night Barry Krupp was murdered, and used it on him?"

No, they both testified. They had been with Rube all night, and both swore Rube had the shotgun with him at all times.

The Sheriff put Rube Calloway on the stand. "Rube, your men testified that they were with you at a camp five miles west of town at the time Barry Krupp was murdered. They said they never left your side, and that you had your shotgun with you at all times."

"That's correct, Mr. Sheriff. My boys wouldn't lie." He laughed heartily at his little joke.

"And you couldn't possibly have left your shotgun at the Green Bull Saloon when you left that night?"

"Nope. Wherever I go my shotgun goes along. It's kind'a like we're married to each other."

"You're sure, Mr. Calloway?"

"I'm dead sure."

The Sheriff reached in his pocket and brought out a handkerchief and opened it. He showed the contents to Rube Calloway. "Do you know what these are?"

"Course I do. Anyone can plain see that's buckshot."

"Notice anything peculiar about this buckshot?"

"Nope."

"Examine them more closely."

Rube's face was suddenly solemn as he studied a few of the lead balls.

"I'll help you if you haven't noticed." Bill handed over two of the lead shots for the Judge to examine. "Doc Grove dug these six shots out of Barry Krupp the night he was killed."

"That right, Doc?" asked the Judge.

"That's right," said the Doc.

"Note there's an X filed on each piece of buckshot. The night you three showed up in town, I had Burl Campbell from the general store open a couple 12 gauge shotgun shells and file an X on each piece of lead, then seal them back up. Doc Grove, Burl Campell, Mayor Ingells and Deputy Bradmiller are all witnesses. We did this together."

Sheriff Bill looked directly at Rube Calloway. "When you gave up your shotgun at the Green Bull that night, I switched shells on you. You and Pate and Drury testified that the shotgun never left your side that night. If that's so, then how do you explain the six pieces of buckshot found in Krupp's body have X's marked on them?"

"We didn't do it!" Pate exclaimed as he jumped up. "He done it! Rube done it!"

"This ain't fair!" said Rube as he flung the shots across the room.

The people in the courtroom broke out in loud voices. Even the jury members were mumbling among themselves. Rube, Pate and Drury were all on their feet, protesting loudly, but their lawyer sat at his table and didn't say a word.

The jury found all three guilty, and a week later most of the town turned out for the hanging. The Sheriff and his Deputy had the honors of putting the noose around their necks.

At the end of the day, the bodies were still hanging from the scaffold, swaying gently now and then when a mild breeze came up. An hour before sundown, the Sheriff and the Deputy pulled up in a dray, cut the men down and laid them in the wagon box. The Mayor, the Doc and Burl Campbell were present for the final ceremony.

Judge Fuhrman, who had been sitting in a chair on the boardwalk and watching the event before him, stepped down from the walkway and approached the five men. He looked at the bodies, stared Sheriff Bill Long in the eyes for a long while, and then looked at the guilt-ridden faces on the other men. "You boys cut them grooves in that buckshot after you dug 'em out of old Barry Krupp, didn't you?"

The silence betrayed their thoughts. Finally the Sheriff spoke. "You knew all along, didn't you, Judge?"

"Course I did."

"Why you asking now?"

"Well, I didn't want to bring it up until after they were hanged."

The Judge turned and walked back to his chair and sat down. He crossed a leg and looked back at the men. "Ain't that a beautiful sundown?"

The five men turned their heads at the same time to take in the view. Then Bill and Len crawled up in the buckboard, snapped the reins and headed for Jake's parlor.

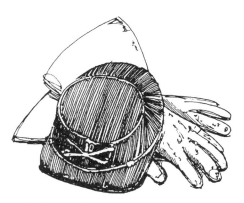

The Man in Between

John Running Wind was the Indian name his mother had given him, but when he joined the cavalry he had enlisted as John Running. No one questioned him or his background, and there was no need to, because he could read and write English and looked more white than Indian. From a distance, however, he could easily pass for an Indian since his skin was naturally dark and his hair was black as coal, but up close his blue eyes and round face spoke of the white blood his father had given him.

John Running spoke perfect Arapaho, a secret he had always kept from his superiors for fear the Indian bloodline might hamper his career. No one knew his father was a mountain man and that he had taken an Arapaho squaw as his wife, a woman who was almost thirty years younger than he was. As a youngster John Running Wind grew up in the wilds of the Colorado Rockies where he had learned to trap for beaver and mink, and where he had learned to shoot deer and elk and bear. In his later years he had lived among the Arapaho in various villages along the western fringes of Kansas and Nebraska with his parents until his father died.

On his deathbed, his father had advised John to experience the life of the white man's culture and then decide for himself whether he wished to continue living among the Indians. It was a fair request, one even his mother encouraged, so John Running Wind had done what his father advised. He had gone east to live among the whites and somehow ended up in the army, where he fought with the North during the last two years of the Civil War. He had earned a battlefield commission and now, seven years later, was a First Lieutenant stationed at Fort Larned, Kansas.

When the commander asked Lieutenant John Running whether he would take charge of the four wagonloads of supplies headed for the Indian agency near Sand Creek, in Colorado Territory, the Lieutenant jumped at the opportunity. He knew that the Arapaho tribe in which his mother now lived was somewhere in the vicinity of Big Sandy Creek and the Purgatoire River.

In all the years John Running had served in the military, he had not once taken official leave. On this occasion when he put in for a month's leave, the request was granted and was to commence as soon as the delivery of the supplies to the Indian agency in Colorado was complete.

No one asked why he asked for leave during this time, and no one really cared.

On the tenth day of September, Lieutenant John Running left the Fort with an escort of twelve soldiers under his command. Four days later the small wagon train passed through Dodge City and six days after that the detail was about to complete the two hundred mile journey.

"Sir," said the young corporal to the Lieutenant as he pulled his horse to a stop. "I spotted the Big Sandy about six miles ahead."

The Indian agency was supposedly only a few miles on the other side. Lieutenant Running gauged the time by the sun, then turned to Sergeant O'Malley, his second in command. "Think we can make it by nightfall?" he asked.

"Absolutely," said the Sergeant. "Just got ta' hustle the boys a bit." He wheeled his horse about and shouted, "Git them mules movin' lads and we'll be drinkin' beer a'fore nightfall!"

The drivers and those on horseback all heard the encouraging words and whooped as they urged the mules on.

The Sergeant nodded his head at the Lieutenant as the two watched the wagons pick up their pace. "Cold beer drives these youngens," he said to the Lieutenant.

The Lieutenant smiled. "Seems to drive you, too."

The Sergeant cackled. "What d'ya say we ride on and have a first-hand look at the river?"

The Lieutenant left a corporal in charge, and the two headed off toward Sandy Creek at an easy lope. They reached the river inside of a half-hour and crossed to the far side. From a hill, they could see a smattering of buildings a few miles ahead and assumed that was the agency. By the time the wagons first appeared on a hill behind them, the Lieutenant and the Sergeant had been able to enjoy a short rest under a lone cottonwood. The sun was rapidly going down, and when the wagon train rolled into the agency it was already dark.

As they pulled up outside the agency post, an older man with a limp came out to see what the ruckus was.

"What the ha'il, interrupting my sleep?"

"Are you Mr. Samuel?" asked the Lieutenant.

"Nope, I'm Emil Harbor. Work for him." He pointed down the near empty street with his thumb. "Mr. Samuel's at the Bird's Inn."

All the Lieutenant could see was the dark outline of a building and a few horses tied to a rail outside. A sudden burst of laughter broke the silence of the night.

Emil Harbor nodded, "That's it."

"They got cold beer down there?" asked the Sergeant.

"As cold as beer gets around these parts," answered the old fellow. "Whiskey too."

The soldiers whooped, and one of them hollered, "Any women?"

The old man looked over the soldiers. "Only two, but I think they can handle this bunch."

The soldiers whooped again.

The Lieutenant got off his horse. "Mr. Harbor, we've got four wagonloads from Fort Larned. Can you sign for them?"

"Shor 'nuff. Have your boys put the wagons in that livery

over there." He pointed to a dilapidated structure across from the post. "We can unload 'em in the morning."

When the Lieutenant looked around, the livery, the Bird's Inn and the post were all that made up the agency. Across from the Bird's Inn, it appeared a few shacks lined the street, if indeed that could be called a street.

"Sure is bleak around here," said the Sergeant as he eyed the same set of buildings.

"Ain't never been no other way," said Emil.

The Lieutenant produced the papers, and in the darkness of the night, the old man signed for the supplies. The Lieutenant then directed the men to take the wagons to the livery, and the old fellow went along with them. "Sergeant O'Malley, set up camp and a perimeter around here somewhere and post some guards. I imagine if you stay a few days, nobody will miss you back at Fort Larned. That should give all the boys a little recreation time at the Bird's Inn."

"Ain't ya about to join us for a beer or two?"

"Nope, I'm officially on leave, so you're in charge." Lieutenant John Running climbed back into his saddle. "See you in a month back at Fort Larned."

John Running headed his horse to the south and rode for a couple hours enjoying the warm, evening air. As long as the moon was full and he could see well ahead, he kept a fairly straight course.

Along about midnight, he came to an offshoot of the Big Sandy Creek, found a spot among some trees and bedded down for the night. At sunrise he was up and made a small fire on which he made coffee. A piece of jerky and some hard tack was going to have to hold him until his next meal, whenever that was.

Instead of dressing in his cavalry uniform, he donned a pair of canvas pants and a shirt, which he carried in his saddlebags. In his bedroll was a light buckskin fringe jacket, which replaced his tunic. He still wore the tan-colored cavalry hat, but took off the military insignia, and then he turned the Army blanket upside down on his horse to hide the blue and yellow cavalry colors. For all practical purposes, he now looked like any drifter crossing the land. The only thing military that gave him away was the U.S. issue McClellan saddle, but even that was not much of a hindrance, since many civilians owned such saddles that had been discarded by the military when upgraded.

John Running was trying to make himself look more like John Running Wind, and although this set of clothes was not at all Indian in appearance, it was the best he could do for the moment. If he was going to venture into Arapaho country, a lone rider, especially one dressed in cavalry garb, was an invitation to trouble.

He set off toward the south again, guessing the Arapaho village might be along the Big Sandy, but as the morning wore on, he had no luck finding a village or even any signs of one. He could have asked Emil Harbor where the Arapaho villages were, but he did not want anyone to know he intended on spending his leave among the Indians.

Close to noon, hunger pangs were gnawing at him and he was now looking about for any game. He had seen deer earlier in the day, which was a prime time to spot them, but now with the hot sun above, even deer had sense enough to find a shady spot to wile away the day.

On a high rise, which presented a spectacular view in every direction, John Running could see the Big Sandy as it wound to the southwest, and along it he thought he spotted a dust cloud of some sort. He took the binoculars from his saddlebags and looked through them at the swirling cloud.

"Cattle?" he said out loud. Someone was driving cattle in this direction. Where there was a cattle drive there was a chuck wagon, and that meant a meal for the offering if he was lucky.

The cattle were at least four or five miles away on the other side of the Big Sandy. John Running rode along the river, found a place to cross and continued on toward the herd, and inside of another twenty minutes he met up with the two cowboys riding point.

"You boys must be a long way from home," said John as he

rode up to the two.

"That we are," said the shorter man. "Might even be lost. This the Big Sandy Creek?"

"It sure is."

"See, Martin," said the other cowboy with him. "Told you this was the Sandy."

The short man spit out some tobacco juice. "Thought we was on the Pergatoire River."

"That's west of here a half day's ride or so," said John.

"Name's Martin Jonason," said the shorter, squat man of the two as he offered a hand. "We're looking for an Indian agency around here run by a fellow named Samuel."

"You're on the right path. 'Bout thirty miles up on the creek."

"That's good to know," said Jonason as he stood in his stirrups and looked off to the north. "Mister, if you can stomach some of Ole's stew, you're welcome to join us. We gotta water the herd for a spell anyway."

As the three headed in the direction of the wagon, John probed the foreman. "You say you're driving these cattle to the Indian agency?"

"That's right. Got a government contract to deliver 300 head. Started in Fort Worth and been on the road about nine weeks now."

While they ate Ole's stew washed down with strong coffee, John gained a little information on the herd. Martin Jonason and his crew had left Fort Worth with a thousand head of cattle. They had delivered four hundred head at Fort Sill and another three hundred at Camp Supply, both in Oklahoma Territory. This last bunch was for the Samuel Agency, part of the winter provisions the government had promised to deliver for dissemination to the Indian tribes on their reservation.

John Running knew these cattle were intended for the Arapahos, but he did not impart this information to the Jonason crew, and he did not tell them he had just delivered four wagonloads of supplies to the agency the day before.

John Running thanked the Jonason crew for their hospitality,
then climbed on his horse and slowly walked through the throng of
cattle as they watered along the Big Sandy. Almost all of the cattle
wore an XT brand, and a few had Circle C's on them.

After he crossed the Big Sandy, he headed west toward the
Pergatoire in hopes he could locate the Arapaho camp before sundown. If the camp was not along the Big Sandy, he guessed it was
somewhere in the hills to the west.

By late afternoon, he reached what he remembered as the
Hills of the Wind, a name the Indians had given this spot. Because
of the configuration of the landscape, a gust of wind traditionally
charged through this narrow draw every day of the year. In the winter, the wind was bitter cold; in the summer it offered a cooling effect, and that was the result now as John led his horse through the
pass.

As he searched the bluffs to either side, thoughts of his youth
came back to him. It had been ten, maybe twelve years since he had
traveled through this pass, but now, as he marveled at the blue grama
grass and wild daisies and the hillside Junipers, he remembered how
peaceful this area had always been.

Those peaceful thoughts came to an abrupt end when, from
out of nowhere, a rifle shot echoed, and a bullet thumped into the
pummel of his saddle. His horse bucked and threw him from his
back. Where he fell the grass cushioned him, and off to the side was
a thicket of wild bushes. He rolled unhurt into the brush and scrambled
beyond a few feet and then suddenly found himself rolling down the
bank of a dry creek bed. At the bottom, he got to his feet and took off
at a dead run.

After a hundred yards or so, he stopped and listened for any
sounds. The shot appeared as if it had come from ahead of him and
to his right, so whoever fired at him must be directly across from him
now, if he was still there.

John carefully climbed up the bank within the shadows of a
rocky overhang. At the top, the high grass gave him the advantage of

remaining fairly concealed. Almost directly across from him he could see two Indians behind some brush and rocks, their attention still focused in the direction where John had gone off his horse. The two men had no idea John had run a hundred yards in their direction. He had his pistol out, but the two were just slightly out of range. With his Winchester rifle, the two would now be heading for the hunting grounds in the sky, but the Winchester was on his saddle and he did not intend to shoot them. Instead he hollered out in Arapaho as loud as he could. "Would you shoot one of your fellow brothers?"

The two turned and ducked down, having no idea where the voice came from.

John hollered again. "I am John Running Wind, son of Henry of the Mountains!"

There was utter silence, then a voice came back, "What was your mother's name?"

"Sun Woman!"

The two Indians stood up in full view. "John Running Wind, it is I, Grey Bull!"

John Running stood up, and the two started walking toward each other. Grey Bull was a boyhood friend of John Running, and when they met they gave each other a big Indian hug. Grey Bull appeared as John had remembered him, a short man with shoulders hunched up like a bull buffalo, from which he derived his name.

"Your aim was not so good," said John. "Your bullet hit my saddle instead of me."

Grey Bull laughed and motioned to his friend. "Little Calf fired the shot, not I. It seems the Great Spirit was good to both of us today." Grey Bull scrutinized John Running's clothing. "You dress like a white man. Shouldn't do that in Arapaho country."

"Do you always shoot at white men?"

Grey Bull's lips tightened as he cocked his head to the side. "There was a time when we didn't, but now-a-days it is hard to trust a white man. Most are better off dead. Are you looking for our camp?"

"Yes."

"It is to the north on the Pergatoire River."

"Is my mother still among the living?"

"Yes, she is. But there are many whom you once knew that are gone now. Come. We can still reach the village before the sun sets."

The three rode off on their horses, and before the sun was down they reached the camp of about forty teepees strung out in the trees along the Pergatoire. As John rode through the village, those that recognized him greeted him, and some shook his hand as he rode past until Grey Bull led him to the teepee where his mother lived.

She was sitting on the outside on the ground in a circle with some other women. John recognized her right away and stepped from his horse. From a few feet away, he looked into her face, but she simply stared ahead as if he were not there.

"She's blind," said Grey Bull. "She was living among the Cheyenne when the blue coats struck the village a few seasons back. A bullet took her sight from her."

John had heard about the Sand Creek Massacre, but he had no idea his mother had lived with the Cheyenne at the time.

"Mother," he said as he knelt down in front of her.

She radiated, her brown eyes sparkling but unseeing, her lips turned up into a longing smile. Her face was wrinkled far beyond what John had remembered, and the crease where the bullet struck across her forehead was the depth of an arrowhead.

"John Running Wind, my son," she said as her hands touched his face. Her fingers moved ever so gently over his eyes and nose and cheeks. "I had a vision some time back that you would visit. It is good." She leaned forward and kissed him on the cheek, and when she did so, tears flowed from his eyes, and she could feel them.

"I'm so sorry you lost your vision, Mother."

She smiled again. "It is no bother. I see you with my heart, and that is good, my son."

———— ♦ ————

Within the next few days, John Running Wind had ample time to renew past friendships and pick up some new ones. Everyone was interested in his perspective on living among the whites, the people who had invaded their Indian lands and cast them upon reservations. Surprisingly most did not seem hostile even though they knew he was a member of the U.S. Cavalry, however, a few voiced concern whether he considered himself white or Indian.

He was wearing a beaded buckskin shirt now, which was a gift from Grey Bull, and to keep his hair in place, he now wore a red headband. He looked every bit as much Indian now as he once had, and it suited him well. What did not suit him well were the complaints of how the white man was treating the tribes. Annuities arrived periodically from various points, but it seemed there never were enough supplies to go around. Flour, salt and dried vegetables were always lacking, and they had received very few blankets during the past winter. The tribes were to receive rifles and ample ammunition for shooting game, but the number of rifles they had been promised never were delivered.

With the scarcity of supplies, the Arapahos had been forced to continually seek game, which they preferred, but it was more difficult to hunt by the old methods of using a bow and arrow. The supplies, when they did arrive, were sent to discourage the Indians from hunting the buffalo, but such a hunt was a tradition from which none of the tribes wished to part. Some small buffalo herds could still be found in the northern Texas and Oklahoma areas, and some roamed the western parts of Kansas and Nebraska. But those lands that the Arapaho once inhabited had been given to the white settlers, and buffalo in those areas were hunted by various other tribes.

"It is not good," said Grey Bull as he and a circle of friends, among them John Running Wind, sat in the shade of an oak. "At one time it would take many days to ride across our land. Our hunting grounds were once the size of a great mountain chain, but now in comparison, we are forced to live on land the size of an ant hill."

The men pondered the fate of not only the Arapaho, but the

Cheyenne and Wichita and Commanche to the south and the various Sioux tribes in the north.

"It is the same all over," complained One Wolf.

"It is time we join together as a nation and defeat the whites," said Crow as he cast a weary eye at John.

John knew, of course, that if all the Indian nations joined together, they could not defeat the whites, but he held his tongue. Such were the complaints and concerns of the tribal members, a recurrent subject that seemed to be the main topic of conversation every day. When John Running Wind told them he personally had escorted four wagonloads of supplies to the agency no more than a few days ago, and that a herd of cattle should have reached the agency by now, their spirits brightened.

At that moment, Little Calf, Grey Bull's friend, rode up and dropped from his horse. "I see by your faces and your comfortable positions under the shade tree that you are once again engaged in political battle."

All of the men laughed.

"I have good news," said Little Calf

Crow's face beamed. "I suppose the supplies are in."

"How did you know?" asked Little Calf.

"The Great Spirit paid us a visit a few minutes ago and informed us. You just missed him."

When Little Calf looked skyward with a blank look on his face, all the men laughed heartily.

"I can't wait to receive my two days supply of tobacco," one of the men said in jest. The men laughed some more.

"And I my handful of beads," commented another. "That should hold me through the winter." All of the Indians including John Running Wind laughed at the sarcasm.

In the morning, several members of the tribe headed off for the agency to receive their supplies, but John chose to remain at the camp and spend most of the day with his mother. It was surprising how well she could sew in spite of having no eyesight. She could tan hides, build fires and cook as well as anyone in the camp.

She lived with one of her brothers whose family treated her very well, and for that, John was grateful. John could not help but feel sorry for her, but if she had any remorse with the loss of her eyesight, she did not show it. She seemed content, and he did not believe she was putting on a show simply to make him feel good. During the day, many of her friends stopped by to talk with her, and this gesture alone comforted John somewhat.

John learned from his mother that Black Kettle was the chief of the Cheyenne tribe that the cavalry had so ruthlessly devastated on the Big Sandy. Many men, women and children died on that fateful day even though an American flag was flying on a pole outside the Chief's tent. His mother had married a Cheyenne warrior some time back, and that was the reason she was present during the Sand Creek Massacre. Unfortunately he had been killed during the foray, and as a result she had returned to her Arapaho village. Since John was a member of the forces that seemed to be pitted against all Indian tribes, none of this discussion sat well with him. He pondered heavily how he could help the matter, but he did not come up with any solutions. His mother felt his sorrow, yet she did not hold it against him that he had chosen the army life among the whites, for she knew he was a good man and a good son.

That evening members of the tribe brought in the supplies which they had picked up at the agency, and when the Chief distributed them to the various families, John Running Wind was on hand. He was close enough to hear the same complaints that once again the tribe did not receive ample blankets for the coming winter and it did not receive sufficient flour and salt to hold them until the next delivery.

Crow singled out John Running Wind and voiced his disgust. "Once again the soldiers have lied to us. What can we do with six rifles?"

"Six?" asked John.

Crow scoffed again. "The whites overlook it when we hunt

buffalo, but the buffalo are almost all gone. And even if we do find a small herd, six more rifles will not help kill many."

Another member scowled. "The whites have delivered us another wagon of lies."

Other members paraded by John, their faces filled with looks of contempt. As John headed back for his tent, Grey Bull caught up with him and tried to console him. "John, my friend, do not take their words to heart. Crow always complains."

Crow had a right to complain, as they all did. "Grey Bull, you received only six rifles?"

"Yes."

"How many rifles did the other tribes receive?"

"Four each."

"How many cattle did your tribe receive?"

"Ninety. The others received seventy each. Why do you ask?"

"Just curious," said John. Although Grey Bull asked him if he would care to join him and some others on a hunt in the morning, John declined. He had other things in mind.

By late morning the next day, John rode in to the Indian agency by himself. He was dressed in his cavalry uniform, and as he walked his horse down the dirt street among the scattered buildings, he noticed only a few Indians sitting outside by a shack in the shade. Three saddle horses were tied up outside the Bird's Inn Bar, and other than that, the community appeared near empty. He dismounted in front of the agency post, and when he entered, Emil Harbor, who had signed for the supplies that John had brought in, was sitting behind a counter. The old man was surprised to see an officer suddenly appear.

"I'm looking for Mr. Samuel," John asked.

Emil Harbor looked the officer over carefully, not sure what to make of the situation. "He ain't here."

"Where is he?"

"Don't rightly know."

"Do you run the place when Mr. Samuel is not around?"

"That's right."

"Good. I'd like to see Mr. Samuel's books."

The old timer gave a snide laugh. "No one sees Mr. Samuel's books without his permission."

John exhibited some patience. "Mr. Harbor, I delivered four wagonloads of supplies less than a week ago, and you signed for them. Remember?"

The man pulled a face, examining John very carefully now. "You were the Lieutenant that night?"

"I was."

"Didn't recognize you. Thought all you boys went back to Fort Larned."

"Not all of us."

Emil Harbor bit his lip and finally shook his head. "Still can't show you the books, not unless Mr. Samuel says so, and he ain't here."

At that moment a scrubby faced man entered the post. "Got a problem here, Emil?" the man inquired.

"Burt, this man wants to see Mr. Samuel's books."

"Nobody sees Mr. Samuel's books, cavalry man or otherwise," Burt answered. "My advice to you is to git."

"I don't take advice very well, especially from a couple of low-down thieves."

Burt lunged at John, but caught a fist in the face that sent him to the floor. The blow caught him totally by surprise, but in a moment he was on his feet. John had his pistol out and slammed the barrel across the side of his face, which sent him back to the floor out cold.

"Jesus!" said Emil as he stared at the blood leaking from Burt's temple.

John eyeballed Emil. "I'll have a look at those books now."

Emil produced a leather bound manual, and John opened it to the last entry where it listed the supplies he had brought in. He skipped over most of the items and read the entries for the rifles and cattle.

"It says here you gave out twenty rifles and three hundred cattle to the Arapaho tribes."

Emil Harbor swallowed hard. "That's right, Lieutenant. I see'd it all given out yesterday. Every bit of it."

"I brought in four wagonloads of supplies. Less than three loads were given to the Indians. Where's the rest of the supplies?" The man on the floor stirred a bit and when he raised up, John kicked him in the head and sent him flat to the floor again.

He turned to Emil Harbor once more, but the man said nothing. "Mr. Harbor, I'm out of patience. I want to know where Mr. Samuel is, and if you don't tell me, you're not going to be very happy when I get done with you."

The old man was shaking in his boots. "I swear, I don't know where he is."

John grabbed Emil by his neckerchief and dragged him around the counter and out onto the street. He marched Emil across to the livery, and once inside he found a rope and threw it over a rafter. He made a loop and stuck it over Emil's head.

"My God, you'd hang an old man?"

"You're damn right. Let's start with the missing wagonload of supplies. Where is it?"

Emil's eyes bulged. "I don't know nothing!"

John pulled the rope and hoisted the man off the ground just inches so only his toes touched the dirt. The man struggled for a moment until John loosed the rope. Emil stood on firm ground and grabbed at his neck, gasping all the while.

"You're also missing about seventy head of cattle. Where are they?" demanded John.

"Lieutenant, I don't have any…"

John jerked him off the ground again, and this time let him dangle for a half minute before he released him. When he did so, Emil fell to the ground, grabbing at the rope about his neck. He gasped and wheezed as he fought to get air into his lungs.

Just as John jerked the man to his feet again, a shot rang out from behind him. John whirled and saw Burt standing in the open door of the barn, a pistol in hand. Just as another shot rang out, John jumped to the side and rolled. He pulled his revolver and fired back and heard the man groan as he dropped to the ground.

By the time John reached the doorway, three men were running in his direction from the Bird's Inn, none of them carrying a weapon. Burt, the man he had whacked in the head at the post, was dead and so was Emil Harbor. One of the shots Burt fired had struck the old man in the chest. In short time, more people had gathered, among them a few Indians and two young ladies, whom he suspected were associated with the Bird's Inn.

John had fire in his eyes as he looked over the crowd. "I'm Lieutenant John Running. I'm looking for a missing wagonload of government supplies and seventy head of cattle. Anybody know anything about that?"

No one answered. "Anybody here work for Samuel?"

Again no one answered. John singled out a short, burly chested man wearing an apron. "What's your name?"

"Alfred Combs."

"You the one that runs that chicken coop inn?"

Alfred nervously stepped back. "Yes, sir."

"Do you own it?"

The man licked his lips and eyed the two men next to him as if searching for an answer. "No, sir. I just serve the drinks. It belongs to Mr. Samuel."

"Who owns this livery?" asked John.

"Mr. Samuel," said the barkeep.

"And all the rest of the buildings in this town?"

"Mr. Samuel," he answered again as he nervously eyed the two cowboys next to him.

John turned his attention to them. "You two also work for Samuel?"

One of the two young ladies, a black-haired beauty, stepped forward and grabbed a cowboy by the arm. "No, they don't." She pointed to the two dead men on the ground. "They worked for him. If you want to find Samuel, he's up north somewhere."

"Where?" asked John.

"Nobody really knows, " she answered. "On occasion he just leaves and shows up a few days later."

"And nobody knows where he goes?"

Alfred Combs, the barkeep spoke up. "Nobody don't ask Mr. Samuel nothing, and that's the way he wants it."

"Mr. Combs," John said as he motioned to the two dead men. "You bury these two no-good thieves, and bury them deep, you understand me?"

"Yes, sir."

John walked outside the livery and beckoned for the three Indians to come to him. In their tongue, he said, "Among the Arapaho I am known as John Running Wind."

They all nodded. "We have heard of you," said one of them.

"Do you know where I can find the agent named Samuel?"

The same Indian pointed to the north. "One of our people once spotted him a morning's ride in that direction. But if you go looking for him, I wouldn't wear the clothes of the blue coats."

John nodded. "Do you know Grey Bull of the southern tribe?"

"Yes."

"Tell him what you saw here today. Tell him two of the white thieves are dead and that I am going after this man named Samuel."

"I will tell him," said the Indian.

———— ♦ ————

By mid afternoon, John Running had covered close to fifteen miles, wearing his traditional Indian clothes to make himself less obvious. On each high hill along the way, he had stopped long enough to scan the surrounding area with his binoculars, and now he was doing the same from a rise that allowed him a good view of the land in all directions. No more than a few miles distant, he spotted three men driving about twenty head of cattle.

He kicked his horse in the flanks and headed in their direction, and as he neared the drovers, all three pulled rifles from their scabbards and rested them across their saddles.

John waved as he approached, hoping the gesture might alleviate their suspicions, but they held fast to their rifles.

"You boys from around here?" he asked as he pulled his horse up.

The man nearest him seemed surprised at the question. "Nope," he said as he eyed John's attire. "Not that it's any of your business."

"Just curious, seeing as how you're driving cattle across the northern edge of Arapaho territory."

The three glanced about them as if they expected Indians coming from every direction. "So we're driving cattle. Any law against that?" asked the spokesperson.

"No, I guess not," answered John. "If the Indians don't mind, I guess I don't."

The man scrutinized John's clothes. "You an Indian or a white man?"

"I'm a white man. Anybody who talks English this good sure as hell ain't no Indian."

The three men laughed and put their rifles away. "Damn, you sure look like one of them savages."

John laughed. "Whenever I ride through their country, I dress like them. That way they leave me alone."

The men chuckled again. "What you doing wandering around here in the middle of nowhere?"

John could plainly see most of the cattle were carrying the XT brand, the same brand the Texans had delivered to the agency. "Looking to buy some cattle. Yours for sale?"

"No," said the man. We just picked up this lot. We buy 'em regular from Jacobson."

John was quick to pick up on the name. "I heard he's got a place around here, but I don't know where."

"Cross the first creek west then head north about eight miles.

Gotta look for a narrow pass off to your left or you'll miss it. That's where Jake keeps his cattle."

"Well, gentlemen, thank you for the information. You watch out for Indians or you're bound to lose your scalps."

They were laughing as they got their cattle moving again.

When John walked his horse past the small herd, he looked over the brands again. A few other brands were present, but almost all carried the XT.

John headed west toward the creek they had mentioned, and when he found it, he headed north and paced himself. Inside of an hour he found the pass that the man had told him about.

Instead of entering the narrow passageway, he tied his horse up in some trees, grabbed his binoculars and climbed up the hillside. At the top, he could see the narrow valley below where cattle grazed along a narrow creek. With his binoculars, he scanned the bottom-land and could see a small shack a half mile away. In front were two horses, saddled and bridled, and alongside the shack was a small corral, which held a half dozen horses. On the far side of the shack was what looked like a combination barn and stable. Whoever Jacobson was, this was a nice secluded spot to hold cattle.

As he scanned the bottomland again, two men came out of the shack and climbed on their horses and headed in his direction. When they were almost below him, he got a good look at the two. One was a lanky fellow dressed in khaki colored clothing. The other was a robust man with a long black coat and a wide-brimmed white hat. His clothing was reminiscent of the attire that one might associate with a southern gentleman. As the two passed beneath him no more than a hundred yards away, the man with the white hat looked up and waved, his gesture aimed at someone on the far side of the narrow opening.

Across from John, no more than a 150 yards, a man stood with a rifle in his arms. John flattened himself and slowly crept backward. He had been in plain sight of the man across from him for some time and was surprised the man had not seen him, but more than likely his focus was on the path below. Obviously the man was guarding the entrance to this valley enclosure.

John crawled behind some rocks from where he could still observe the man across from him and still have a view to the open lands to the south. In short time, the two that had passed below him had urged their horses into a trot and were now heading in the direction from where John had come. Who they were, he did not know, but he guessed the robust man with the white hat may have been the agent, Samuel.

He again turned his attention to the enclosed valley and focused his binoculars on the cattle nearest him. There was no doubt these were from the same bunch the Texans had brought up from Fort Worth. Somewhere along the way these cattle had been cut out from the main herd.

For the next fifteen minutes, he sat patiently out of sight of the man across from him and while he did, he carefully scanned the ridges that encircled the small enclosure. He could see no other men posted anywhere and was satisfied that this narrow pass was the only entrance, and he figured that was the reason the guard was posted here.

As soon as the sun began to dip beyond the horizon, the man across from him made his way down the hill, and in seconds he emerged from some trees on his horse and rode back to where the buildings were. Since he took the saddle off his horse and corralled him, John figured he was in for the night.

John picked his way down the hill and carefully made his way to the corral back of the shack. By now, a lamp was lit inside and light came through the windows.

He skirted past the corral, and although he could see three saddles sitting on a fence nearby, he still was not sure how many men were inside the shack.

He ran across a short open area to the barn where he entered through a side door. Inside it was still light enough to see a wagon sitting in the middle of the building. He pulled back a tarp, which revealed several crates. He risked striking a match and was not at all surprised to see the U.S. Army symbol stamped on each of them. He knew at a glance that the longest crate of the bunch contained Spencer rifles, all meant for the Arapaho villages.

The agent known as Samuel had a good set-up. From this secluded spot, no more than twenty some miles from the agency, he could peddle all the goods he pilfered from the Army. John wondered how long he had been doing this, and how many thousands of dollars worth of supplies his own people had been cheated out of. The anger he now felt caused him to shudder. He left the barn and crossed quickly to the shack where he looked through one of the windows. There were only two men at a table, but both were armed.

The anger still raged inside of him as he silently walked around to the front door. He paused for a moment, and then with his pistol cocked, he kicked in the door.

The two men were so startled, they jumped up and reached for their guns. John fired four shots before either could clear their holsters. One of the men jerked backward against the wall and ended up sprawled out face down. The other slowly slumped to the floor. John knew the man against the wall was dead, but the man nearest the table was holding his stomach where blood was pumping out of him. John knelt down next to him and propped his head up.

"You kilt us," the man mumbled.

"I wouldn't have if you didn't go for your guns. I'm looking for Samuel."

The man grunted. "You just missed him."

"Was that him, the man with the long coat and wide-brimmed hat?" The man stared back at John, his eyes open, but he never heard the question.

John went outside, saddled one of the horses and headed back to where he left his own horse. He had some hard riding to do if he was going to beat Samuel back to the agency.

———— ♦ ————

It was close to midnight when Samuel and his lanky partner, Courtney, returned to the agency. While Courtney put the horses in the livery, Samuel entered the agency post. Usually a lamp was burning, but the post was dark tonight, which he found strange. Samuel groped in the dark, found a lamp and lit it.

"Emil?" he called out. "Emil, Burt, you here?"

Samuel searched the sleeping quarters at the back of the agency, but the room was empty. It wouldn't be unusual for Burt to be at the Bird's Inn, but Emil rarely went to the bar.

As soon as Courtney returned, the two walked to the Bird's Inn. A small crowd of cowboys and drifters were hanging around the two girls when the men entered, but their merriment came to a standstill when they saw Samuel and Courtney standing in the doorway. Alfred Combs was behind the counter, his eyes flashing back and forth between Samuel and the man off to his left. Samuel saw the cavalry officer sitting by himself at a table in a darkened corner.

"Looking for Emil and Burt?" asked the Lieutenant.

Samuel eyed the military man as he and Courtney slowly crossed the room to the bar. A few men who were with the girls abruptly left the bar, a few remained.

"Might be," answered Samuel with a slow southern drawl. "Know where they are?"

"Buried down deep where all the thieves at this agency belong."

Samuel stiffened, looked at Alfred, who nodded his head.

John went on. "Seems every time government supplies and cattle are delivered, the Arapahos come up short."

Samuel gave a laugh of contempt. "You'll have a hard time proving that."

"I don't think so," said John. "I just came from Jacobson's place. Course, Jake and his buddy are dead, just like you scum suckers are going to be."

Courtney was the first to draw, but John had his Colt on his lap already cocked and pointed in his direction, and when he fired, the bullet tore into the man's stomach and spun him around. Alfred raised a shotgun from behind the bar, but John's Colt barked again and sent a bullet into his chest. The impact reeled him backward, and when his shotgun went off, the blast tore upwards ripping through a hanging lamp. Samuel had just pulled a pistol from a shoulder holster and fired it aimlessly as the kerosene spilled over his coat and set him in flames.

When the man hollered out, John felt a bullet tear into his shoulder that almost wrenched the pistol from his hand. He thought sure another bullet would charge into him, but now, Samuel was screaming as he fought to get the flaming coat off. His big frame slammed into the back bar, and he fell to the floor where a few liquor bottles had dropped and shattered. More flames engulfed the big man and spread burning alcohol all along the wood planks. Those men that were still in the room grabbed anything they could and tried beating out the flames of his clothes, but in seconds the entire back of the bar was in flames and the heat was intense. More horrific screams burst from Samuel's lungs as the flames seared his flesh.

John looked down at the man, and when he saw the pleading eyes on his blackened face, he cocked his pistol and fired point blank into Samuel's chest. Samuel slumped down and didn't move.

"Everybody out!" someone shouted.

John was the last to leave. Outside, everyone that lived within the community had gathered a safe distance away, all gaping as they watched the Bird's Inn go up in flames.

"John Running Wind," said someone in the crowd.

John turned to see Grey Bull at his side. "You are wounded," he said when he saw blood leaking from his tunic. He helped John slip off the coat, then pulled his shirt back and examined the wound. He simply nodded. "The bullet went right through. You will be okay." With that, Grey Bull folded his arms in front of him and once again stared at the fire.

By dawn the building was nothing but a smoldering ruin of black, and the only remaining observers were John Running Wind,

Grey Bull and three other Arapaho Indians.

In time, John knew he would have to ride to Fort Lyons to the south and send a wire to Fort Larned, but for now, he and Grey Bull climbed on their horses and headed in the direction of the village.

Mr. Jenkins' Property

"Just passing through, Mr. Jenkins?" asked Burton McKillip. McKillip dealt out the last round of cards, picked his up, looked at them and quietly turned them face down.

"I'll take three," said the gentlemen to his left.

"Me too," said the next man.

"Yes, I am," said Jenkins, the new face at the table. "I'll take two."

Burton McKillip dealt out the cards. "Ever been to Coal Ridge before?" he asked.

The first gentleman threw his cards in. The second raised twenty-five dollars.

"No, first time," Jenkins answered. "Twenty-five and fifty more to you, sir."

Burton McKillip raised an eyebrow. He had been at this table most of the afternoon and was down almost eight hundred dollars. One of the men playing at the table had two hundred of his money, and Mr. Jenkins had the rest. McKillip put the seventy-five in the pot, the other man folded.

Jenkins turned over a pair of queens and watched as the southern gentleman quietly tucked his cards under the deck. "What might be your line of business?" he asked as Jenkins collected his winnings.

"Cattle buyer."

"Where would you be purchasing cattle in these parts?" asked McKillip. He took a long, slender cigar from his inside vest pocket and lit it up. As he did so, one could not help but see the gold ring with a glittering stone on one finger. Burton McKillip was slender like his cigar, with long fingers. He was immaculate in appearance with a thin, black mustache on his gaunt face. The flat, wide-brimmed hat he wore, whether at the tables or not, was his calling card. He was easy to recognize from three hundred yards away.

"I ain't buying cattle in these parts," answered Jenkins.

In comparison to McKillip, Jenkins was a squat man with a squared off face and a bushy handlebar mustache. He was wearing a western-cut suit with a white shirt and string tie. His boots were shiny new, but his hat, scuffed and dark around the sweatband should have been thrown away a year ago. As far as Burton McKillip knew, the man was not carrying a weapon.

Burton McKillip was in the habit of sizing up the men he played cards against. He figured this man to be about forty, and figured him to be a good family man. He guessed the man probably had two or three sons who were good with cattle.

"Do you have a family, Mr. Jenkins?"

"No, I don't. Never married."

So much for that observation, Burton McKillip was thinking as another round of cards was dealt out. He had been reading this man wrong for the better part of the afternoon. Maybe that's why he hadn't been reading the man's cards right either.

Burton McKillip looked at his cards and calmly turned them face down. "Texas?" He asked.

"What's that?" asked the cattleman.

"I wondered if you were headed for Texas. To purchase cattle, that is."

"I'll take two," said the first gentleman.

"Nope. I'll take three," said Jenkins.

Burton McKillip took one card, the dealer took three.

"Bet," said the dealer.

"By me," said the first gentleman.

"Fifty," said Jenkins as he shoved five ten-dollar coins into the center of the table.

Burton McKillip and the dealer called the bet, but the first gentleman folded.

"So, I take it you already bought your cattle?"

Jenkins laid down three deuces and collected his winnings as the other two quietly shoved their cards under the deck.

"That's right."

"What brings you to Coal Ridge?" Burton McKillip asked.

"It's on the way to St. Louis."

"Ah, yes. You do have that distinct St. Louis accent."

"My sister lives in St. Louis. I was born and raised on the Niobrara River in Nebraska."

Burton McKillip pursed his lips, gave a slight frown of displeasure in guessing wrong again. "That's a long trek on horseback."

"That it is. However, I'm traveling by buckboard."

Burton McKillip did not see a buckboard parked outside when he entered the saloon. He assumed the buckboard was at the livery.

"Staying at the hotel, are you, Mr. Jenkins?"

"Nope. I got nothing against sleeping under the stars."

That meant he was probably going to travel later on, Burton McKillip was thinking. He looked at his watch. It was near four o'clock.

The four men played on another hour. One of the men left the table, but another took his place, and as they played Burton McKillip occasionally ordered a round of drinks for the table. Jenkins had had four straight whiskeys, and still the money was stacking up in front of him.

A few onlookers had stopped to watch the men play, most of them surprised to see a cattleman taking money from one of the best card players in southern Arkansas. If Burton McKillip was angry that his cards weren't turning a profit, he didn't indicate it. A half-hour later the cards still weren't leaning in McKillip's favor. Then finally, on a hand in which McKillip held three queens, the betting became heavy. McKillip pushed a hundred dollars into the center of the table, the last remaining money in front of him. Jenkins, a poker-faced player if there ever was one, saw the bet and raised three hundred.

The bystanders now were talking in low voices, amazed at the amount of money on the table. They waited anxiously for an answer when Jenkins asked, "Are you going to call, Mr. McKillip?"

The southern gentleman stared at his cards. Three queens was a good hand, and he had a lot riding on the table, but he had no more money. "Will you take a note, Mr. Jenkins?"

"No, I won't," answered the cattleman without any hesitation.

"I'm good for it."

"I'm sure you are, Mr. McKillip. But when I sat down, I believe you gentlemen set the rules, and I believe you said cash only. Did I misunderstand you?"

Those that heard the comment nodded their heads, talked among themselves. The house rules had always been cash, and those watching the game knew it and so did McKillip.

The southern gentleman took a sip from his whiskey and stared into the eyes of his opponent, trying to read something more, and trying to work himself out of the dilemma. He definitely had a winning hand. "Would you accept property?" he asked finally. "Property is as good as cash."

"Not unless you have the property with you," Jenkins said with a wry smile. The small crowd looking on pressed in closer, their attention drawing to a peak.

"Well, I do have it with me," said McKillip. He nodded at one of the men in the crowd who left the saloon. In less than a minute, the man returned to the table, another man with him.

Now the crowd murmur heightened even more as Burton McKillip introduced the man. "This is Jeremiah. He's strong as an ox and is certainly worth three hundred dollars."

Mr. Jenkins stared at the black man, a tall fellow with husky shoulders. There was no doubt this man could do the work of two, but to use him on a bet?

"He's reliable and trustworthy, and he would never lie to his owner."

Jenkins was still stunned, but he tried not to show it. Although he did not approve of slavery, he did not intend to make an issue of it, not here in slavery territory. He was careful with his choice of words.

"Mr. McKillip, are you serious? Using a man as your bet?"

"He's my slave, Mr. Jenkins. I own him."

Jenkins still had his doubts. How could anyone use a man in place of cash, and still in good conscience consider himself a gentleman?

McKillip went on. "You did say if I had the property *with* me, did you not Mr. Jenkins? Jeremiah is my property, he's with me and he's worth every bit of three hundred dollars. There isn't anyone in the house that would disagree." McKillip looked at the crowd seeking confirmation.

"He's worth it," said one.

"No doubt about it," said another. "He's a good worker."

More people gathered around the table now, wondering how the cattleman would react.

Jenkins was very matter of fact. "All right," he said. "I'll accept your word he's worth three hundred, and if it's your custom to bet people at the tables, I'll go along with that, too."

Burton McKillip smiled. "Would you like me to put him on the table, or is it all right that he remains standing here?"

Laughter filled the room.

"He can stay where he is," said Jenkins as he turned over his cards. He had three sevens and two deuces.

The full house beat McKillip's three queens. He didn't even bother to show them as he threw up his hands. "Well, Mr. Jenkins, looks like you just won some property."

Jenkins stood up, looked over the big, black man he had just won. He was a handsome looking fellow and dressed in heavy denim work clothes. The cattleman gathered up the money he had won and said to McKillip, "Thank you for an enjoyable afternoon of cards." He motioned to his newly acquired property. "Come along, Jeremiah."

The two walked out of the saloon and crossed the street to the hotel. "You got a last name, Jeremiah?"

"Yes, suh. Jeremiah Jefferson."

"You hungry, Mr. Jefferson?"

Jeremiah smiled. No one had ever addressed him as Mr. Jefferson before. "Yes, suh. I am."

"Well, then let's get something to eat."

"Suh, I can't go in there," said Jeremiah as Jenkins started into the hotel.

"Where I eat, you eat," said Jenkins as he grabbed Jeremiah by the arm and led him into the hotel lobby. He spotted the restaurant sign, which led to the dining room, and entered, Jeremiah right behind him.

Those who were seated at various tables stared at the cattleman and the black man as they sat down. Jeremiah looked about, his face laden with a sense of fear. He knew many of these people and they knew him, and he knew he was very much out of place.

"Sir," said the waiter to Jenkins. "We are not allowed to serve his kind in this establishment."

Everyone in the room had their eyes fixed on the cattleman now.

"What kind is that?" asked Jenkins. The waiter did not know how to respond. Jenkins went on. "I tell you what. I'm not accustomed to your culture and ways down here in Arkansas. You're going to have to forgive me for that, and perhaps this one time you could overlook my ignorance."

He stood up, removed his coat and exposed a .44 nickel-plated revolver in a shoulder holster. "We'll have two of your largest steaks with all the trimmings and a bottle of your best, red wine."

The dinners came inside of ten minutes. Jenkins could not remember having a quieter meal in all his life, and the meal was delicious in spite of the gawking crowd of patrons.

They left the hotel and headed for the livery where Jenkins had left his buckboard and horse. The livery was at the end of the street, and although there were a few buildings between it and the hotel, the buildings seemed to be boarded up. Several horses were concentrated in front of the saloon where Jenkins had spent most of the afternoon, but other than that the street was pretty much deserted.

When the two entered, his buckboard was inside and his horse was in a stall. The proprietor was nowhere about, which surprised Jenkins, since he said he would be here at precisely seven o'clock, and it was exactly that time. Jenkins loosed his horse and set it in place in front of the buggy and began to hitch him up.

"I can do that for you, suh," said Jeremiah.

Jenkins had never had a man offer to do his work for him, but he could see the determination in the black man's face. "Go ahead."

The man knew his work. His hands were quick and strong as he swung the horse collar up in place and trailed the side straps back to the wagon. It was strange to own a man, something that Jenkins had a hard time adjusting to.

"Jeremiah, I don't quite know what to do with you."

"Suh?"

"Have you lived in Coal Ridge all your life?"

"Most of it."

"Did McKillip treat you well?"

Jeremiah hesitated. "As well as any of the other slaves."

The answer didn't quite tell Jenkins what he wanted to know. When Jeremiah reached Nebraska he would be a free man, so Jenkins guessed the man would want to go with him. Still, he gave him the option. "Would you regret leaving here, or do you want to stay?"

"That's for you to say, suh."

Jenkins nodded. "Okay, we'll go to Nebraska. Do you have any belongings we can pick up, or is there anything else you'd like to do before we leave?"

"Yes, suh. I'd like to say goodbye to my family if I could,

suh."

"You've got family here?"

"Yes, suh. My wife Delia and a son, Daniel."

Jenkins removed his hat and ran his hands through his hair. "Whoa," he said as he slapped the hat against his leg. "I can't take you away from your family."

The door rattled behind Jenkins, and when he turned around two men stood in the doorway, one with a rifle pointed at him, the other with a club in his hands.

"Mistah Colder!" exclaimed Jeremiah.

As they neared, the man named Colder spoke. "Jeremiah, you get on out of here and close the door when you leave."

Jeremiah hesitated.

"Git, damn you!" the man snarled as he stepped closer. He raised the rifle and pulled back the hammer, the weapon still pointed at Jenkins.

"Hey, boys, ain't nothing we can't settle peacefully here," said the cattleman.

"Shet up!" hollered the man with the rifle. The man next to him held an axe handle in one hand and was thumping it up and down into the palm of his other. There was no doubt in Jenkins' mind that the man planned on using it.

"Git on back to the plantation, Jeremiah, now!" the man hollered again.

These men were from McKillip's plantation, thought Jenkins as he eyed the man with the rifle.

Jeremiah had a piece of leather harness in his hand, and as he walked past the man named Colder, he lashed out and caught the rifle with a downward thrust. Colder cursed as his rifle discharged into the ground.

The second man raised the axe handle and was about to thrash Jeremiah with it when Jenkins fired his .44. The slug caught the man in the shoulder and spun him around to the ground.

Colder had a single shot carbine and had no time to reload.

He dropped the rifle and ran for the door, but Jeremiah caught hold of him and whirled him around. The man swung some light blows in defense, but he was no match for Jeremiah's bulk. Two heavy punches brought Colder to his knees, and when he made a feeble attempt to get up, Jenkins slammed the gun barrel of his revolver across his head and split it open. Blood spurted as the man fell face down into the dirt.

The proprietor of the livery stable was at the door and had just witnessed the foray. He stared at the two men lying on the ground. Colder was out cold, the other man was groaning mercilessly as he held his bloodied shoulder.

"You got any law in this town?" Jenkins barked at the livery owner.

"No, sir. There ain't no law within fifty miles of here."

"Well, we're going to make history today. Get some water and throw it in this man's face and get him on his feet."

"Yessir!" said the stable owner as he disappeared out back.

"Jeremiah, you and I got to talk."

"Yes, suh."

Fifteen minutes later, Jenkins entered the saloon alone where he had first met Burton McKillip. The southern gentleman was at the same card table, and when he looked up, he had a most surprised look on his face.

"Well, Mr. Jenkins. Back to play some more cards?" he asked. There was a slight waver in his voice when he spoke.

"Maybe. Got a few other things to settle first."

"What did you have in mind?"

"I understand two men named Colder and Henderschott work for you." There was fire in his eyes when he spoke, and McKillip could see it.

The room began to quiet down as those nearby listened in on the conversation.

"I do have two such men working for me. I don't believe that's any secret."

"Mr. McKillip, for a southern gentleman, you're a damn poor loser when it comes to cards. Do you normally send out hired help to do your dirty work?"

McKillip pulled away from the table and was about to stand up. Jenkins had his .44 out and the hammer back before the man could blink. "Stay seated if you want to remain healthy.

"Jeremiah!" he hollered without turning around.

Jeremiah and the livery proprietor came through the saloon doors bringing Colder and Henderschott with them. Both had their hands tied behind their backs, both were a bloody mess.

McKillip's face went pale when he saw his men. He forced himself to recover. "Mr. Jenkins, we don't cotton to you northerners coming down here and meddling in our affairs."

"I don't call it meddling when two of your men try to kill me."

One of the men next to McKillip inched his hand off the table to his side. Jenkins fired a shot in the center of the table that blew chips and coins up in the air. "You two boys at the table take your weapons out easy like unless you want to spend the rest of your short life wishing you had."

The two men, friends of McKillip, knew the cattleman meant business. They put their revolvers on the table and pushed their chairs back.

"Now, Mr. McKillip, I'd like you to put that .32 caliber pistol you carry inside your coat on the table."

"I can assure you, Mr. Jenkins, I'm unarmed."

"Not according to Jeremiah. He says you are, and I believe you told me he wouldn't lie to his owner."

The cattleman stuck the .44 against McKillip's chest, then reached inside his coat and pulled the revolver from its place. "Now, ease that derringer out of your boot, if you will."

McKillip cringed as he lifted the derringer from its place and put it on the table.

"Back where I come from, you and these two bloody skunks

would be strung up by morning."

The threat was real. "Mr. Jenkins," said McKillip as he placed his hands flat on the table. "I'm sure there's been some mistake here. There must be some other way we can resolve this."

"That's the first smart thing you said today," said Jenkins. He could see some relief cross the man's face when he spoke. "I understand Jeremiah has a wife and son who are still at your plantation. Property, as you call it."

McKillip nodded. "That's right."

"What do you figure that property is worth?"

"One hundred fifty dollars."

"I'll wager that amount. Deal me one card, deal yourself one."

McKillip looked over the crowd, then looked at the cattleman knowing he had no choice. He shuffled the deck and dealt one card to Jenkins and one to himself.

Jenkins turned over his card. It was a four.

McKillip eased his card up. He had a jack. He put it back face down and said, "You win."

That did not surprise Jenkins. He knew he had a win-win situation. Those in the room broke into a loud murmur, and several nodded their heads indicating it had been a fair bet.

Jenkins looked sternly at McKillip. "I'll thank you to send for my property right now if you don't mind."

Burton McKillip nodded at one of the men at the table.

"Jeremiah, you go along with him," said Jenkins.

"Now, Mr. McKillip, I'd like you to make out a bill of sale for my newly acquired property. I've been told that will make the transfer of ownership legal in these parts."

Someone produced paper and ink for McKillip, and every man in the room looked on as he wrote out the bill.

Jenkins took the paper from him and put his revolver away. "I'll be at the hotel if anyone needs me." At the door, he turned and addressed the saloon crowd a final time. "Next time I come through, it'd be a good idea if you had some law around here." The cattleman turned and stomped out of the saloon.

In the morning, just after sunrise, Jenkins and his property pulled out of town. "What do you know about cattle, Jeremiah?" Jenkins asked his new hand.

"Not much, suh."

"Can you ride a horse?"

"Yes, suh."

"We'll teach you the rest. Mrs. Delia, I hope you can cook."

"I can, Mr. Jenkins, suh." Her eyes flashed with excitement.

"We'll keep you busy at the ranch house. Always plenty to do around the Nebraska sandhills. And I'll pay a fair wage to you both." Jeremiah and Delia had never been paid a wage.

Jenkins looked at the boy. "How old are you, young man?"

"Eleven, suh."

"You a good worker like your pa?"

"I can do chores, suh."

"That's good enough. Have you ever had a horse of your own?"

"No, suh."

"Well, a couple weeks from now, we're going to get you one."

The young boy's face beamed as he looked at his father. "Does he really mean it, pa?"

"I believe he does, son."

Jenkins turned to Jeremiah. "You ever been to St. Louis before?"

"No, suh."

"Neither have I.

"Come on, Lucky!" he said to his horse as he snapped the reins and set him into a trot.

A Stop at the Cold Spur Inn

The Wichita Agency wasn't much of a town. In its heyday, which lasted no more than a few years, it served as an Oklahoma Territory Agency for the Wichita Indians, from which it derived its name. The Cheyenne and Arapaho were strung out along the Washita River, and the Commanches lay to the south, other tribes that were to benefit from the white man's intrusion upon their lands.

The agency was abandoned after the war, and the town now, at best, was occupied by a few diehards, whose only attraction rested with Morgan's Trading Post and the Cold Spur Inn, the only saloon within a hundred miles where a man could get a cold beer. The men who came through were mostly cowboys pushing herds north to Kansas and Nebraska. A couple ladies of the night also drew in the cowboys and drifters, but rarely did any of these ruffians leave their horses at the livery, so old man Peterson was close to folding up his business.

In addition to the post, the livery and the saloon, a half dozen smaller buildings held up by clapboard siding, lined a dirt street no more than two hundred yards long. Here and there a few Indians from the Wichita tribe, mostly dressed in black coats and floppy hats, sat in the shade of the overhangs, the only respite from the heat of the hot summer sun.

Hap McCann and Frank Belleview rode their horses down the street at a slow pace, their clothing covered with dust, sweat rings circling their collars and armpits. Both wore Colt revolvers and carried Henry rifles on their saddles. A bedroll was tied behind each of their saddles along with a rain slicker, which was common for those moving about. They weren't sure where their next stop would be after this one. All they knew was they were tired and beat from doing some hard riding. They had left Tahlequa some four days ago with a posse in pursuit. They figured the posse was at least a day behind them, and they needed a break.

Frank Belleview had stopped at this anthill of a community in prior years when he was riding trail herd. He knew the town, if it could be called that, and its reputation for harboring those who had a habit of living on the wrong side of the law.

This was all new to Hap McCann. "What are we doing in a god-forsaken hole like this?" he asked as he looked over the desolate surroundings.

"Not much, other than a bath and a shave and a cold beer at the Cold Spur. You for that?"

"I'm for anything that will get us out of these saddles for a few hours."

Frank laughed out loud. "And we might just hustle up a couple little gals. I'll introduce you to Miss Connie, who I'm sure you will enjoy, and I for sure will enjoy Miss Prairie Rose."

"You must have come here a lot."

Frank laughed again. "We all did."

"Well, first things first," said Hap. He climbed off his horse at the trading post and tied the reins to a railing.

"What say we get a cold beer first?" asked Frank.

"Nope, boots first." He held up his left boot and showed Frank the open toe where the seams had torn out. Then he lifted his right boot, which had half of the sole missing. Frank grunted as he stepped from his horse and mumbled his displeasure as he followed Hap into the post.

Morgan Weatherford was big and burly chested with a long growth of beard. He sat behind a counter at a table sorting some papers when Hap and Frank entered, and although he looked up, he didn't offer a greeting. Frank eased himself into a wicker chair and waited while Hap walked around the store.

The post provided an assortment of staples, which included flour and beans and other drygoods, as well as clothing and blankets. Boots and other cowboy ware and a few saddles and bridles filled one section. Another section was devoted to heavier tools, among it, shovels, pick-axes and building supplies.

Hap was drawn to a wall lined with several Sharps rifles and two .50 caliber buffalo guns. A chain ran through the trigger guards and was padlocked at one end. Not one new rifle was displayed, and those that were were in sad shape.

Hap found a pair of brown high-topped boots and measured the soles against his own. He was mildly surprised to find them made of good quality leather, and better yet, they were his size.

He browsed some more, and as he walked around the store, two Indians rode up on painted horses. One waited with the mounts while the second came inside. He was wearing a light colored buckskin vest and had matching leggings. A turquoise colored band rimmed his forehead and held his hair close to the sides of his face. His skin was unusually dark, but the most prominent feature was his nose, which was crooked as if it had been broken. In spite of the bent nose and some deep scars on his face, he was a handsome looking man.

The Indian waited in the doorway for several seconds, looked cautiously first at Frank, then at Hap, then stepped directly to the counter. He loosed a string of mink pelts from his waist that were tied together with a leather thong, and as he lay the pelts on the counter he pointed to a jade-green, beaded medallion and chain.

When Morgan Weatherford got up from behind his desk, he was even more of a giant than Hap had thought before. He had to be well over two hundred fifty pounds and towered over the Indian. The Indian spoke in his native language and again motioned to the chain hanging from a nail on the wall.

Morgan answered him in his own tongue, and after a somewhat heated conversation, the Indian grabbed his pelts in disgust and left the store.

"I told the son-of-a-bitch ten pelts the last time he was here," Morgan grumbled, as if Frank or Hap cared. "Eight don't cut it. And besides, never did like him."

Hap approached the counter. "What's a white man's price on that necklace?" he asked.

"One dollar," the big man snapped.

Hap put a dollar on the counter. "I'll take it."

Morgan smiled. "Tell you what, cowboy. You put that chain around your neck and go parade around that Cheyenne buck out there a couple times, I'll give it to you. There's nothing I'd like better than to see the look on his face when he sees you wearing it."

"It's a deal." Hap dropped the necklace over his head and walked outside. The two Indians were still standing next to their horses when he approached them. Hap turned to see Morgan at the window with his eyes wide and a grin on his face. Putting on a grand show, Hap paraded back and forth in front of the Indians and once again glanced back at the window. He could hear the burly man bellow with laughter.

Then Hap took the necklace off and pointed to the eight mink pelts the Indian was holding. The two exchanged the items and the trade was made.

When Hap came back in the store Morgan was seething in anger. "What the hell?" he barked.

Hap picked up the leather boots he had been looking at earlier and lay the eight pelts on the counter. "Nice doing business with you."

The big man shoved a hand in Hap's chest and stopped him short. "Just what the hell you think you're doing, cowboy?"

"Making a trade. Eight pelts for a pair of boots." Hap pointed to a chart on the wall behind the counter. It listed the value of a horse, a buffalo robe and the number of mink, ermine or beaver pelts required in trade for a variety of items. Eight mink pelts would buy a pair of leather boots.

Hap started to exit, but the big man grabbed him by the shoulder and spun him around. "Just one damn minute! You cheated me!"

Hap drew his pistol so quick, Morgan had no time to react. He jammed the pistol into Morgan's neck and shoved him back against the wall. "You calling me a cheat?"

Frank was suddenly on his feet. "Now, Morgan, your sign says eight mink pelts buys a set of boots."

"You stay out of this, Frank," the man barked.

"If I stay out of this, Hap's liable to take your head off." Frank grabbed Hap's arm and eased his gun down.

Morgan glared at Frank. "You two get the hell out of here." The words came threatening through clenched teeth.

Outside, Hap and Frank grabbed the reins of their horses and started leading them to the Cold Spur Inn.

"Damn," said Frank. "That was real sweet. Ain't too many people get the best of Morgan. He's a tough old buzzard. He could knock you down with a gob of spit."

When Hap looked back at the post, Morgan was on the porch staring back at him.

"He looks mean," said Hap.

"Yeah. He's got a temper. Ain't got too many friends either, and those that are his friends ain't anybody else's friends."

"I take it you two bumped heads before."

"Some years back a few of us came through here and got a little liquored up at the Cold Spur. Little Billie Weiler, his first time on a cattle drive, ended up dead. We were sure Morgan done it, so a couple of us came over and beat him up. We would have killed him if some of our hands hadn't pulled us off.

"We all loved little Billie. Good sense of humor, no more than sixteen or seventeen."

A dray with a matched set of blacks sat outside the saloon, and in front were a few saddle horses. The two tied up their horses next to them, and Frank waited while Hap tried on his new boots.

"Good fit," he said as the two entered the bar.

A few men sat at a card table in one corner, drinking beer. In another corner, three men sat playing cards. Hap and Frank went to the bar.

"What'll it be?" the barkeep growled in a not too friendly manner.

Frank looked around. "Where's Roman?" Roman was the owner.

The barkeep pointed with his thumb. "On the hill."

That meant Roman was in the graveyard.

"What happened to him?"

"Got shot."

"Who owns the place now?"

"Morgan. You want something to drink or not?" the man asked, a constant scowl riding his face.

"Two beers," said Frank as he put some money on the bar. "And tell Prairie Rose Frank's here."

"She's gone."

"Where to?"

"Don't know."

"What about Connie?"

"You boys interested in drinking or asking questions?"

Frank grabbed the barkeep by his hair and slammed his face down against the bar. The man yelled out as blood spurted out of his nose.

"I asked you nicely what happened to the girls, now you tell me nicely what happened to them."

The man was shaking. "When Morgan took over, they both left. That's the truth."

"Who shot Roman?"

"I don't know! I swear, I don't know!"

"Did Morgan shoot him?"

The barkeep was silent. Frank jerked his hair again.

"Please, mister, I don't know nothing!"

Frank released his grip. "Next time I ask you a question, you be polite, you understand?" He turned to the other men in the room. "Anybody here know who killed Roman?"

No one answered.

Frank and Hap sat at a table with their beers. The rest of the men in the bar were now back at their cards and drinks.

"Nothing I hate more than some smart-ass bartender that thinks he something more than a bartender," said Frank. He looked around. "Things sure have changed. No piano, no girls any more. I doubt if we could even get a bath. There used to be a dozen or more cowboys in here all day long." He sipped at his beer. "At least the beer's still cold."

The two heard a door slam, and when they looked up, the barkeep was gone. When the two finished their beers, the barkeep still hadn't returned, so Frank pumped two more for Hap and himself and sat down again.

Sometime later the door slammed in the back and the barkeep came in and went directly to his station. Frank eyed him curiously, then glanced through the window. From up the street he could see Morgan coming with three other men.

Frank went to the bar and gave the man a hard look. "Roman used to keep a sawed off shotgun behind the bar. I'll take it now, if you don't mind."

The little man was shaking, but he didn't respond.

"Unless maybe you'd like a bigger lump on your nose." The barkeep reached down and brought up the shotgun.

Frank returned to the table and sat down. When Morgan and his three buddies entered, Frank had the scattergun out of sight under the table with both hammers cocked. The three men with Morgan weren't as big as he was, but they looked just as mean, and they wore pistols at their sides. Frank knew Morgan usually kept his pistol under his buckskin jacket in his belt.

Morgan snarled. "Henry said you roughed him up a bit, maybe broke his nose, and that ain't nice, Frank."

"Well," said Frank. "A man that lacks manners deserves to get his nose broke." He looked at the barkeep. "Right, Henry?"

Frank was cocky now. "You should be more careful of the bartenders you hire. Henry just told me how you acquired the Cold Spur. He said you killed Roman, shot him dead."

Morgan jerked his head at Henry.

"I didn't tell him nothing Morgan! I swear, I didn't say nothing!"

Frank was fishing for another answer now. "He said you killed little Billie Weiler, too. Remember little Billie, Morgan?"

Henry was shaking more than ever. "Morgan! For chrissake, I didn't say nothing!"

Morgan twisted his face at Frank. "You're talking pretty big for a fellow who's about to have his head blowed off with a shotgun."

Frank smiled. "What shotgun might that be?"

Morgan eyed Henry, nodded his head slightly at him.

"You killed Roman and little Billie, didn't you, Morgan?"

Morgan and the three men reached for their weapons at the same time. When Frank loosed both triggers on the shotgun, the blast splintered part of the table away, most of the buckshot ripping into one of the men. Gunshots erupted from both parties now. Hap's shots found their marks. The second man managed to fire, but his bullet went directly into the floor. The third fired a wild shot as he went down, his bullet shattering a window. Morgan hadn't even been able to get his pistol out of his belt when Frank blasted away. In no more than ten seconds, Morgan and the three men were sprawled out dead as dead could be. By now, those at the card tables had flattened themselves against the floor.

A cloud of blue smoke waved across the room as the onlookers slowly got up and made their way for the door.

"Stay where you are, everybody!" Frank commanded. All the men froze in place, their faces full of fright.

Frank looked at Henry, the bartender. "Morgan killed Roman and little Billie Weiler, didn't he?"

Henry slowly nodded his head.

Frank looked over the crowd of men. "I'm guessing a few of you men knew Morgan was a killer, and I ain't holding it against you that you didn't speak up. There's a posse after us, probably no more than a day behind. The two of us are wanted by the law for cattle rustling and a few other things, but we want you to know we ain't killers. When the posse shows up, you tell them that. You tell them what happened here. Will you do that for us?"

"Yeah," said one of the men.

"Yep," said another. Then all the men nodded they would comply.

Frank placed some money on the counter. "Henry, give everybody a drink on us, and make it your best whiskey."

"Yessir!"

As the men crowded up to the bar, a few mentioned that Morgan finally got what was coming to him, and that the town would be better off without him and his ilk.

Frank Belleview and Hap McCann walked past the bodies on the floor and went out of the saloon on to the boardwalk. The street had the same deserted look as when they first arrived. Then, on the horizon a good mile and a half away, they both saw the eight or ten horsemen coming their way.

"Damn," said Hap to Frank. "They're closer than we thought."

The two men climbed into their saddles, spurred their horses and rode off as fast as they could.

Harker's Hill

Jesse saddled up and rode off to Dickinson with all the speed he could muster out of his five year old mare, pressing the animal, knowing that time was of the essence. He reached the small town by early evening and summoned Doc Wielding, then borrowed a fresh horse from his good friend, Sam Beaker, to ride the eighteen miles back to his ranch ahead of the Doc.

When Jesse arrived it was late, and standing in the doorway was his wife, her thin frame silhouetted against the light coming from inside the log home. Jesse dropped from the saddle and feared the worst.

"He's gone," was all she said as she slowly sank to a bench on the porch. A bright moon shone so brilliantly, illuminating the yard, it's light reflecting off the roofs of the few buildings. Jesse sat down next to her, wrapped an arm around her and comforted her by pulling her tightly against him. They sat quietly, saying nothing, listening to the night sounds that darkness brings, until their silence was interrupted by the rumble of Doc Wielding's buggy in the distance. Within a few minutes the Doc pulled up in front, wrapped his reins and stepped down bringing his leather satchel with him.

Doc Wielding was a small man in his fifties, always wore a dark suit with a white frock shirt and black string tie, but now he was wearing a light coat on top to ward off the cool of the night. A glance at the two told him immediately little Samuel had died. He walked directly into the home to the crib in the corner and looked down at the young one. He pulled Samuel's night shirt up and carefully examined the body, turned him over to view his back, then spread Samuel's hands open to check the palms. He was examining the bottoms of his feet when Jesse and Helga came up behind him.

"Bring a lamp," he asked in a soft voice. With the light shining directly above the crib, he carefully opened little Samuel's mouth, and depressed the tongue with an instrument.

He put the instrument back in his bag and sat back on a chair and thought for a few moments. "When did this start?" he asked.

Helga simply stared at the child expressionless, as if she did not hear his words, and then in an almost inaudible voice, she said, "Yesterday he seemed restless, then this morning I noticed a rash on his body. Then came the fever. He wouldn't eat."

Doc Wielding dipped his head, ran his hand up to his chin and stroked his beard for some time. "The others?" he asked.

She pointed to a door that led to an adjoining room, then picked up the lamp and headed for it, Jesse and the Doc right behind her.

The other two youngsters were in separate beds, Erica, six years old, little Jesse ten. A quick examination revealed both with chills, and each had scaling on their palms and feet. The Doc knew that before morning they would break into a fever and their bodies would eventually be covered with a heavy rash

"What is it?" she asked.

The Doc looked directly into her glazed eyes, then into Jesse's sorrowful expression. They both knew, but he said it anyway. "Scarlet fever. The chills will turn to a fever, and when that comes, soak towels with cold water and cool them down. In the morning make a strong soup. Their tongues will swell and their throats will be sore, but you must get them to take nourishment."

Helga's face sagged even more, and suddenly she broke into sobs. Jesse held her tightly, tried to console her, and when her knees buckled, he picked her up and laid her on the bed.

"I'll stay the night," the Doc said. He returned to the main room, removed his coat and rolled up his sleeves, and while he was washing his hands, Jesse came into the room. Helga's heavy sobs penetrated the home, and Doc Wielding could see the pain in Jesse's face. "I'll give her something to calm her down." He wiped his hands dry with a towel, stood pensively for a moment, and then in a quiet voice said, "It doesn't look good, Jesse. I think you better prepare for the worst."

Jesse sank exhausted into a chair. "What is it Doc? I already have two on the hill from the small pox, and now this. Why our children?"

Doc Wielding knew Jesse well, knew he was as strong as an ox, big and burly, and able to work from morning to night without taking hardly a moment's rest. But Helga had always been a frail lady, small in stature, extremely thin, and though she had born five children in her short lifetime, all the births had been tough ones. On two occasions Helga had nearly died.

"Jesse, you've got a wife who's never been real healthy." He paused. "Many children this age manage to come through all right, whether it's small pox, scarlet fever or whooping cough. But your children just don't seem to have a very good immune system."

The Doc shook his head. "I guess it's God's way of doing things. I don't pretend to understand it all."

Doc Wielding stayed for two days, and then helped Henry dig graves for the three little ones. Now there were five markers on the hill.

No one else had attended the burial, other than the Doc. A day later Sam Beaker, from the hotel in Dickinson, rode out with his wife to pay his respects, and the same day Pete and Elvira Mansfield, their nearest neighbors, arrived in a dray. Towards evening Sam Beaker and his wife left, as did Pete, since he was a rancher and had cattle to attend to. Elvira stayed on to console Helga during this heavy period of mourning, but she too, having a family to attend to, returned home after a few days.

Helga's deep depression never left her, thus she spent most of her days sitting on the porch bench, staring off to the south toward the open range land, oblivious to the hot, piercing sun. Jesse worked his cattle, checked the waterholes for any that were bogged down, but never strayed too far from the home place. He always managed to work his way back every few hours to check on Helga, and quite often he would find her sitting on the hill next to the graves of her children, softly rocking back and forth, singing a lullaby. On those days when her depression seemed at its worst, he remained on the home place and either dug more fence post holes or repaired his barn, or spent his time working on anything else that required some attention. He tried to involve her in daily chores, but she had no spirit, no will to do anything but mourn her family.

One late afternoon Henry rode home on his mare simply to check on his wife, and when he came into the yard, Doc Wielding's buggy was in front of the house. Jesse dismounted and was about to walk in the house when he noticed the Doc in the doorway of his barn.

Jesse hurried across the yard, saw the remorseful look on the Doc's face.

And then beyond the Doc, Jesse could see clearly through the open doorway of the barn where the shadowed figure of his wife was hanging from a rope.

Jesse's knees weakened and he slowly sank to the ground. "My God," he said as the life drained from his face. "She did it."

Exactly two weeks from the day they had buried the children, Jesse and Doc Wielding dug another grave on the hill.

———— ♦ ————

The hill had always been a landmark. In this fairly flat country, this huge mound rose majestically out of the ground as if some medieval force had erected it. Jesse had heard that more mounds like this were common a hundred miles to the west. On top of this particular mound were a few small trees, and this was where Jesse had buried their first two children a few years ago. Now all of his family were on the hill. Like some giant ant hill on the prairie, this protrusion was visible from several miles, and those who passed within a few hundred yards could easily see the six wooden markers Jesse had made for the graves.

And because this hill was a piece of land on Jesse Harker's ranch, and more perhaps, because his entire family was buried on top of it, people began to refer to the mound as *Harker's Hill.*

In the first few months following Helga's death, Pete and Elvira would occasionally drop by, not necessarily to offer consolation, but simply to visit Jesse with a genuine concern for his welfare and to determine how he was handling the loss of his family. They were mildly surprised to see how well he had adjusted, and in so short of time. Each visit, Elvira would bring a few loaves of bread or a freshly baked pie, or some other baked goods that a man running a ranch might crave from time to time.

And so it was, that Pete and Elvira Mansfield left on each occasion with the assumption that Jesse was handling the tragic loss of his family quite admirably. Whenever Sam Beaker, the owner of the Dickinson Hotel paid a visit, he too thought Jesse was adapting well to his situation. Privately they were all convinced Jesse was as strong mentally as he was physically, and that he had come through the tragedy quite well.

But unknown to any of his friends, there were may times while Jesse was checking his cattle astride his dun mare, that a moment out of his past would strike him, and he would feel the pain inside. Each time he held back his tears, and after a few minutes he would gain his composure. His thoughts were constantly on his family, and now that he had no family he realized much he loved each and every one of them. Helga, as frail and as sickly as she had almost always been, nevertheless, was a very devoted wife and an extremely attentive mother.

Over the course of time, his sorrow began to work on him, and he kept reminding himself that perhaps he had never spent enough time with each of the children. He wished he had taken them to town more often so they could have enjoyed other children of their ages, could have become familiar with things other than the simple ranch life that surrounded them.

This piece of land and the 150 cattle he was raising seemed to be all he worked for day and night. But now that his family was gone, the herd meant very little to him.

As time went by he began to neglect the cattle, neglect his chores on the home place. In summer the sun could be penetratingly brutal, so quite often in midday Jesse simply stopped working and would spend time on the top of the hill, sitting in the shade of the few trees, enjoying what breeze came by off the plains. He had begun to spend so much time on the hill that he eventually dragged a rocking chair to the summit along with a small table on which he could rest a bottle and a shot glass.

Eventually, even when the days were not so terribly hot, he began to find restitution from misery on the hill and sometimes would spend hour after hour during a perfectly nice day, simply rocking back and forth, smoking his pipe and sipping at his whiskey.

————— ✦ —————

August came, and it had been raining for three days straight. The creek that ran past the ranch place was overflowing and even threatening the grounds around the buildings. Even now, as Jesse sat under the trees in his rocking chair on the hill with his slicker and wide brimmed hat sheltering him, he seemed oblivious to the pelting rain that found its way through the foliage from above. It was morning, and though he was clad in a wool shirt and a light jacket, he constantly tugged at the slicker about his throat to keep in the warmth.

He was staring off across the river to the south, not thinking about anything in particular, when a voice startled him.

"Jesse, what in the hell are you doing up here?"

The words were so unexpected, Jesse jumped from his chair and in the process lost his balance and fell to the ground. The table next to him tumbled, and with it came a half filled bottle of whiskey thudding to the ground.

Pete Mansfield stood just a few feet away, soaking wet in his slicker, his hands holding on to the reins of his saddle horse.

"Are you drunk?" asked Pete. He was a big man like Jesse, and had a scowl on his face that would have stopped a charging bull.

Jesse Harker slowly got to his feet and had to work hard at keeping his balance once he was erect. He stared downward, ashamed to look Pete in the eye.

"My God," said Pete as he looked over the stack of whiskey bottles. "Most of your cattle are way south of my place and you have a half dozen calves floating down the river. Ain't you in the least bit concerned?"

Jesse wavered on his feet and managed a glance at Pete and then lowered his eyes again.

"And where's your mare? I checked the barn and all your horses are gone."

Jesse motioned with his hand. "Out there somewhere."

"Are you all right, Jesse?" Pete asked as he made a few steps forward.

Jesse stared into his face, and suddenly the tears rolled out of his eyes. He pointed at the grave markers, his voice broken. "They're all gone, Pete. What'd I do to deserve this?"

Jesse cried so hard, he dropped to his knees.

"Oh, God, I'm sorry!" said Pete as he knelt down and grabbed Jesse by the shoulders. He hugged him tightly and let Jesse cry it all out. "This ain't your fault, Jess. Ain't none of this your fault."

After a few minutes, Pete helped him to his feet. "Come on, let's get you back to the house."

Inside the log cabin, Jesse put on the coffee, and while he was getting cleaned up, Pete left on his horse and came back a half hour later with Jesse's mare. Their breakfast consisted of coffee and some hard sourdough buns.

"Feel up to riding?" asked Pete once Jesse had settled down.

"I guess so."

"I'll get my two oldest ones and we'll get your cattle back where they belong. Elvira's got pork steak on for supper. You feel

up to that?"
"I do."
"Good. Come on. Let's saddle up your mare."

———— ♦ ————

A week slipped by for Jesse Harker, but the days were long. He was back to working a full schedule again, riding the range and on occasion working on the buildings in the ranch yard. Keeping busy sixteen hours a day seemed a good routine. He purposely tried not to think about his family, thinking that if he exhausted himself during the day, he would sleep soundly through the nights. But living on his small ranch alone was not easy. He was not much of a cook, something Helga had always attended to, and he was not much for keeping up the inside of the cabin. He had to wash his own clothes, and he had shirts and socks that needed mending, and he was sorely in need of company. Occasionally Sam Beaker from town dropped in, and periodically some passerby would drop in, usually asking for directions. Rarely did anyone stay for any length of time. His neighbor, Pete, had cattle and farmed a good size spread besides, and since he had plenty of work to do, Jesse did not expect him to drop everything and pay visits.

Jesse's mother had died when he was only six, and when his father died, Jesse had come out to the Dakota Territory from Ohio, where he still had one sister. The only information he had heard about her came in a letter several years back from an uncle who said she had moved to St. Louis with her third husband. Jesse had only one brother who died when he was three, so the only relatives left in Ohio were some aunts and uncles, and it was very possible none of them lived in Cincinnati any more.

All these thoughts were going through Jesse's mind while he dug post holes to extend his corral. He was also thinking about what Pete Mansfield had suggested when he dropped in the day before.

"Why don't you take a few days off and come into town, Jesse?" Pete had said. "You ain't been coming in regular. Got a lot of friends who miss you."

Jesse mulled over the word *friends*. It wasn't quite the same now without Helga and the kids. Deep inside he felt a bitter resentment, as if those who were closest to him now seemed to be patronizing him. It had been five months since he lost his family, and he could go five more months, five more years, fifty if he had to, and a trip into town wasn't going to change anything.

Jesse had many things on his mind, especially the ranch and the cattle. He had been doing some figuring over the past week, and now his mind was whirling with numbers. He stopped working for a moment, looked across the river at his land to the south, glanced at the hill where his family was buried. More thoughts raced through his head as he returned to his work and nailed a pair of boards in place. He stopped, looked at the sun and judged it was mid morning. It was going to be a hot day.

He abruptly put away his tools in the barn, went to the cabin and washed up and put on a clean shirt. Back in the barn, he threw the saddle on his mare. "We're going to town, Rosy. What say you to that?"

Rosy only responded by swinging a head to the side when he tightened the cinch on her. In moments, Jesse tied his coat and slicker on behind, put his Winchester in the scabbard, swung up into the saddle, and headed down the road at an easy lope.

Inside of a few hours he arrived in Dickinson and went directly to the livery stable where he put his horse in a stall and unsaddled her. While he was giving her some hay, Charlie Gorman, the proprietor walked in.

"Well, talk about strangers," said Charlie as he stuffed a gob of tobacco in his cheek and rolled it around with his tongue until it was in place.

"Hi, Charlie. What's the cattle price in Bismarck?"

"'Bout the same. Some figure it will be up three to four dollars a head by the end of the month, though."

"Oh, why's that?"

"Little winter kill on some of the bigger outfits north of the Hills last year. Ain't as many cattle come through as the yards expected. Why you asking? Figger on selling some of your cattle?"

"All of them," answered Jesse.

Charlie hooked his thumbs under his red suspenders. "Well, now ain't that something. How many head you got?"

"One hundred sixty six. Counted em' yesterday."

Jesse pulled his Winchester from his scabbard and started out of the livery. "Do you suppose they have a room or two left at the hotel?"

"Ain't never been full yet," answered Charlie. "How long you planning on staying?"

"Long enough to find somebody to buy my place." Jesse started walking out of the livery.

"What are you going to do?" Charlie hollered after him.

"I don't know. Maybe go dig for gold somewhere." Jesse left the livery and walked along the boardwalk toward the hotel, satisfied he had decided to leave his horse at the livery. He had no plans to dig for gold, but if he was going to sell his cattle and his ranch, Charlie was the best advertising a man could expect for nothing.

By six o'clock Jesse had checked in at the hotel, stopped at the auction house to inquire about cattle prices, bought the latest paper from the newspaper office, then went to the Heart Saloon and had a couple drinks where he caught up on the latest gossip about the town. Not much had happened in the past few months, he learned. Surprisingly not one of the men he talked to even mentioned the loss of his family, and when he left the saloon he didn't know if he should feel hurt or whether his friends were just trying to be polite and not bring up the subject. Either way, it bothered him and at the same time reinvorced his decision to sell the ranch and cattle as a good idea.

He made his way back to the hotel restaurant where he ran into Doc Wielding, who also was about to order an evening meal, so the two sat down together.

"How you doing, Jesse?" asked the Doc.

"Doing good."

"Heard you were selling your ranch and cattle."

Charlie was working the town well. "Yes, I think I'll sell it all."

"Sure you want to do that?

"Yep."

Doc Wielding could feel a bitterness in the short answers he was getting. "Where you plan on resettling?"

The question was an obvious one, but it took Jesse by surprise, since he had not given much thought about where he would relocate. "Ohio," he finally said.

"Ohio?"

"Or maybe Billings."

Doc Wielding smiled. "First east, then west. You sure you've thought this out?"

Jesse knew his mouth was hanging open. He hadn't thought much about it, but he was saved from answering when a lady approached their table and told them they had their choice of steak, pork or chicken.

Both ordered steak, and when she was gone, Doc Wielding persisted. "Are you serious about selling your place?"

"Reasonably."

"But you don't even have a place in mind where you're going."

"Doc, there's nothing holding me here anymore."

Doc Wielding straightened up in his chair, puffed up his cheeks and blew out some air. He knew Jesse had gone through a terrible ordeal, but he also knew relocating was not the answer to his troubles.

After dinner the two talked at length about everything except Jesse's decision to move off his place, and around eight o'clock, the Doc excused himself, saying he was going to retire early. When he was gone, Jesse produced the paper he had purchased earlier and began reading.

92

"More coffee?" It was the lady who had taken his order earlier.

"Please, if you don't mind."

As she poured the coffee, Jesse looked around the eating hall and realized he was the last customer.

"No need to hurry," she said when she noticed his concern.

"I don't want to hold you up, ma'am."

She smiled. "It's no bother," she said as she headed back to the kitchen.

Jesse finished reading the paper, left his money on the table and walked into the hotel lobby. Elmer Jacobson and Curt Mobring were sitting in a corner smoking cigars when he entered, and after both greeted him, he joined them. They had both heard he was putting his ranch up for sale and moving to California.

"California?" asked Jesse. "Who told you that?"

"Hector at the newspaper office."

"I wonder where he got that notion."

"Ol' Charlie down at the livery said you were going to look for gold."

Jesse laughed. That made sense why he was supposedly going to California. If anyone was looking for gold, that's where they seemed to go.

The three talked for another hour, and when Elmer and Curt left, Jesse decided to retire. He had business to attend to in the morning before he returned to the ranch, and daylight came early.

He had checked in early in the afternoon with Eric Kingsley, a young fellow who sometimes helped Sam out. Sam Beaker was the proprietor and one of his best friends, but now as he approached the desk, he realized he had not seen Sam all day. He stood at the counter for a few moments, looked around, then rang the bell. Almost immediately, the same lady who had waited on him in the restaurant appeared.

She seemed as surprised to see him as he was to see her.

He offered a smile. "Seems like you're working every place

I turn. Where's Sam and Katherin?" Katherin was Sam's wife.

"They left for Bismarck on Wednesday's stage. They'll be gone for a few weeks."

Jesse simply looked at her and studied her a bit. He hadn't paid much attention to her in the restaurant, but now as he stood across from her, he realized she was a fairly short lady, a bit stocky, yet she always seemed to carry a warm smile. She also appeared somewhat overdressed, he thought, for someone working in the restaurant and kitchen. She was wearing a white apron, but her attire underneath was more in the flavor of a house dress rather than that of a matron.

"I'm Sam's niece." she offered. "He asked me a few weeks ago if I would run the hotel for him while he was gone."

"I see," said Jesse. "I guessed you were not from around here."

"I'm from Miles City."

"I see." Jesse was silent for a bit, even feeling a bit awkward. "Well, it's been a pleasure meeting you, ah..."

"Florence. Florence Friedrich."

Jesse nodded, and headed up the stairs.

"Sir, your key?"

He came back a few steps and held out his hand.

She smiled again. "Your room number?"

"Fourteen."

She took the key from the pigeon hole behind her and quickly glanced at the register. "You're Mr. Jesse Harker?"

"Yes," he said as he took the key from her.

"Nice to know you, Mr. Harker."

"Thank you." He nodded and made his way up the stairs.

———— ♦ ————

Doc Wielding was up early the next day sitting in front of the sheriff's office on the boardwalk having his third cup of coffee. Sheriff Halverson's little fat frame filled the chair next to him. The only thing threatening about the Sheriff was the .32 nickel plated pistol in the leather holster that hung in front near his groin. But the way the sheriff was sitting, his belly hung over the pistol obliterating it from view.

As the two sat admiring the peaceful morning, they could suddenly hear the churning wheels of a wagon and the familiar ring from the harnesses of a span of horses.

"Sounds like Pete coming," said the Sheriff.

In short time, Pete Mansfield came around the corner in his dray and pulled up in front. "Morning Doc, morning Sheriff," he said as he got down from his wagon. "I see you two are taking your jobs real serious."

The two men laughed at the comment. "We're resting up for tonight," said Sheriff Halverson. Saturday night was usually when the rowdiness took place. "Soon's the fightin' gets started, someone's bound to get hurt. The Doc will patch them up and then I'll lock them up."

All three laughed. "Seen Jesse?"

"Yep," said Doc. "He's up and about, been over at the livery this morning trying to round up some cowhands."

"Cowhands? What for?"

"Said he's going to sell his cattle. He's looking for hands to help move his herd to the Bismarck cattle pens."

"The hell you say. When did this all come up?"

Doc Wielding and the Sheriff explained what they knew, which wasn't very much, but that Jesse had decided to sell his ranch and the cattle.

"I never thought he'd do that," said Pete. "Did Sam go to Bismarck?"

"Yep," said the Doc.

"Jesse check into the hotel?"

"Yep. Just like you said he would."

Though Pete had suggested Jesse take a few days off and spend Saturday and Sunday in town, he wasn't really certain Jesse would take his advice. But he had, and if Jesse were to overnight, Pete knew he would stay in Sam Beaker's hotel, since he was a good friend of Sam's. That was exactly what Jesse was doing, except Pete had no idea he was planning on selling his ranch.

"This is a damn fool idea, his selling the place," said Pete. Both men agreed. "Got any more coffee?"

While Sheriff Halverson went inside to get a cup, Pete sat down next to Doc Wielding. He slammed a fist down on the table. "Damn, we've got to put a stop to this."

———— ♦ ————

Amos Blomberg finished filling out the paperwork. "Let's see, got the acreage, got the section information." He adjusted his spectacles and looked over the remaining information on the form. "Got an asking price?" he asked Jesse.

"No, leave that open."

"Got an acquisition date?" Jesse didn't know what that meant. "About what time do you want to sell?"

"Don't know. Got to sell my cattle first."

"When will that be?"

"Don't know for sure. I haven't had any luck finding hands yet."

Amos stared at Jesse, more confused than ever.

"Just put things sort of open-ended, Amos. If you find a buyer, we'll deal with it then."

"Right."

"Might want to advertise it in some surrounding papers."

"Right."

Jesse left Blomberg's real estate office and walked directly to the stable where he saddled his horse and left town.

———— ♦ ————

Doc Wielding was in the lobby of the hotel where he had been sitting since five o'clock reading the paper. He had read every word in the gazette and had checked his watch once again, wondering whether Jesse was ever going to return. Jesse had not checked out of the hotel, so Doc guessed more than likely he had not gone home. Charlie did not know where he had gone either, only that he had left in the early afternoon, and had not taken his Winchester with him.

At half past six, Jesse came walking through the door and went directly to the hotel register where he picked up his key from the attendant. He had not bothered to even look around the hotel lobby, rather stomped up the stairs two steps at a time and was out of sight before the Doc could even beckon him.

Inside of ten minutes, he came down the stairs and spotted Doc Wielding in the corner.

"Hey, Doc. Having dinner again?"

The two sat at the same table they had eaten at the day before. Doc Wielding spent some time scrutinizing Jesse's attire, thinking there was something different about his clothes, but these were the same clothes he had on earlier. He sniffed the air. "What's that smell coming off of you?"

Jesse rubbed his face. "Like it?"

"Smells like flowers of some sort."

"Lilac," said Jesse. "Supposed to smell like lilac."

That was what was different on Jesse, the Doc finally realized. Jesse was smelling like a flower and the curls on the back of his head had been chopped off. He not only had a fresh haircut, but a shave too, and he may well have had a bath besides.

"Had a bath too," said Jesse. "Ain't had a warm bath in six months."

Doc nodded, pleased to hear that.

"Went out to see the Hanson brothers . They said they can help me drive the cattle, maybe get Henry to help. That would make four of us."

"Four ain't enough to drive 150 head to Bismarck."

"Hundred sixty six," Jesse corrected.

"Got spare horses, someone to run a chuckwagon?"

"Not yet, but I'm working on it."

"I heard you talked to Amos Blomberg."

Jesse made a face. "You seem to have a lot of interest in my cattle and my ranch. Fact is, everybody in town does. Sheriff Halverson, Charlie. I even talked to Pete Mansfield this afternoon. He acted as if I was crazy or something, selling everything off. Pete said he was here last week, and now he's here again. What's he doing in town two weeks in a row with his buckboard? And without his family?"

Doc Wielding sat back in his chair, not sure how he should respond. Of course they were all concerned about Jesse's welfare. None of them thought it was a wise idea to suddenly pull up stakes.

"We have steak and meatloaf tonight, gentlemen," said the matron. Florence Friedrich poured each of them a cup of coffee. "Hello, Mr. Harker," she said with a smile. "What will it be tonight?"

"Meatloaf, please."

The Doc ordered the same, and when she left the table, he said, "She didn't say hello to me. Didn't even get a smile from her."

Jesse chuckled. "Well, Doc, could be she prefers the company of young fellows like me rather than old farts like you." He was still eyeing her as she headed for the kitchen. "How old do you figure she is?"

"She's twenty-eight."

Jesse looked curiously at the Doc.

"That is, I'd guess she's about...twenty-eight. She's new here, you know."

"That's what I understand, from Miles City. Florence Friedrich is her name. Sam's niece. What's Sam doing in Bismarck anyway?"

"Don't know. Business trip I'd guess." Doc Wielding was silent for a moment, then, "You got a hankerin' for this gal?"

Jesse's face flushed and he straightened up in his chair. "I don't hardly know her."

The Doc raised an eyebrow. Jesse had a haircut and a shave, was smelling pretty like one of the gal singers in the Heart Saloon, and he had had a bath. All in one day.

"What are you grinning about?" asked Jesse when he saw the silly look on Doc's face.

Doc suddenly turned somber. "Nothing in particular. Just wondering how long it was going to take for that meatloaf to get here."

They were just finishing up their meal when Henry Perkins came through the lobby and hurriedly made his way directly to the Doc.

"The Sheriff said you better come quick. The Hanson boys got in a squabble with the Garnesons in the saloon and they're in tough shape. One of em' may have a broken arm."

"Drag 'em over to my office," said the Doc to Henry. "I'll be there soon's I get this last forkful."

———— ✦ ————

Jesse went along with the Doc, concerned that if the Hanson boys were beat up too badly, they wouldn't be able to help him with the cattle drive. One of the brothers did indeed have a broken arm and the other had a slice in his right leg a foot long, which indicated maybe he had been raked by the rowel of a spur. Both of the Hanson brothers' faces looked like someone had taken a club to them, they were so covered with blood. But once the blood was wiped away, the damage wasn't near as bad as the Doc thought.

"If we'd had another five minutes in there," said Frank, the older brother, "we could'a took em."

The Doc shook his head, and in a very serious tone said, "Another five minutes in there and you two would have been fattening Caleb's coin purse."

Jesse laughed out loud. Caleb Halloway was the undertaker.

In less than a half hour, the Hanson boys limped out of the Doc's office, crossed the street and got on their horses.

As they rode out Jesse commented, "It's gonna be a while before they heal up. I might have to find somebody else to help me run the herd."

When Jesse turned to the Doc, he could see a wide smile on his face. "There you go grinning again. What are you so jovial about all the time?"

"Oh, nothing. I've patched them boys up a half dozen times already. You'd think they'd learn." That wasn't at all what the Doc was thinking.

Jesse spent the next few hours at the Heart Saloon where he drank a few beers with some friends, and along about ten he ambled back to the hotel. When he entered, Florence Friedrich was standing behind the counter reading a newspaper.

Before he could even say anything, she said, "You left your meal without having your coffee."

"I guess I did," he said.

"I saved you a cup if you'd like it now."

"I'd like that," said Jesse unhesitatingly. He watched her until she disappeared into the kitchen, and when she returned, the smile on her face was just as warm as the cup of coffee.

———— ✦ ————

Jesse woke fairly late, but in short time he was dressed and down at the lobby desk. No one was present, so he dropped off his key and walked out into the fresh air and made his way down to Sheriff Halverson's office.

The Sheriff usually had coffee on, and this morning was no exception. Doc Wielding and the Sheriff were already working on their fifth cup, he guessed

"Pretty quiet on the streets this morning," said Jesse.

"That's the way I like my Sundays," said the Sheriff.

Jesse hadn't realized it was the sabbath. An hour later people starting walking by on the streets, which meant church had let out.

Jesse spotted Florence Friedrich walking across the street and guessed she was headed back to the hotel. In order not to make his moves so obvious, he drank the rest of his coffee and five minutes later made an excuse to leave the Sheriff's office.

The Sheriff and Doc both knew what he was up to, and a half hour later, when both were on the boardwalk still nursing a cup of coffee, a buggy pulled up in front of the hotel. Jesse climbed out of it and quickly ran into the hotel, and in moments came out with Florence Friedrich. Doc Wielding and the Sheriff watched as he helped her onto the seat, and in a few seconds the horse and buggy had turned the corner and were out of sight.

"Well, ain't that an interesting turn of events, Doc," said the Sheriff.

"Yep," answered the Doc with a huge grin.

———— ♦ ————

One week later, on a Friday, Jesse Harker once again came into town, this time driving his own buckboard with his big, black stud pulling it. Doc Wielding and the Sheriff were already settled in with their coffee when they saw him coming down the street.

"Jesse," hollered the Doc as he motioned for Jesse to drive over. Jesse halted his buckboard in front of the Sheriff's office.

"Mornin' Jesse," said the Doc. "Got time for coffee?"

"No, afraid not. Got some business to attend to. Maybe later on." With that he smacked his lips together signaling his black to move on.

"Bet we don't see him for coffee all day long," said the Doc.

"Bet you're right," agreed Sheriff Halverson.

For the most part of the day, Jesse wasn't visible anywhere in town. Later in the day, Charlie confirmed for the Doc and the Sheriff, that Jesse had approached him saying perhaps he was a little hasty in considering selling his herd. Charlie also learned Jesse had paid a visit to Amos Blomberg at the real estate office, where he told Amos to hold off on placing any advertisements to sell his ranch. Up to that point, Amos hadn't placed any anyway, so it didn't make any difference.

On Sunday morning, the Doc and Sheriff Halverson were at their usual perch when they spotted Jesse and Florence Friedrich come out of the hotel and slowly make their way along the boardwalk on the opposite side of the street.

"Looks like they're headed for church," said the Sheriff.

"Yep," agreed the Doc. "Don't think I've ever seen Jesse in a suit before." An hour later the two watched Jesse and Florence return along the boardwalk, but for the rest of the day, Jesse was conspicuously not present. Towards early evening, Doc and the Sheriff saw Jesse return with his buggy and watched with interest and approval as Jesse escorted Florence Friedrich into the hotel. Moments later he emerged from the lobby, crawled into his rig and drove right past the Sheriff's office with a huge smile on his face. He never gave the slightest hint of noticing the presence of either of the two men sitting in their chairs. At the edge of town Jesse hustled his black into a fast trot.

"Looks like he's headed home," said the Sheriff.

"Yep. Bet next week, Friday, he's back."

"I ain't gonna bet on that one."

———— ♦ ————

On the next Friday, Jesse arrived early in town, once again driving his buckboard. Half way down the main street, he could see Sam Beaker standing on the front steps of his hotel. Sam's tall and lanky frame and thick white hair made him recognizable from a half mile away. Jesse pulled to a halt, simply sat on the seat of his buckboard and stared at Sam. He knew Florence had agreed to work in the hotel while Sam was in Bismarck, but now that Sam was back, it crossed Jesse's mind, that perhaps Florence for some reason had returned to Miles City.

"I see you're back from Bismarck," said Jesse, unable to think of anything else to say. He jumped down from the buckboard and offered Sam a hand. "Good to see you."

"What brings you to town on this fine day?" asked Sam.

It was a loaded question, and Jesse was sure his face couldn't be any more blank as he contemplated an answer.

Sam went on. "Heard you were putting your ranch up for sale."

"I thought about it."

"Change your mind?"

"Well, no, I just put it off for awhile." Jesse looked down at his feet and kicked his heels together like some little kid who had been caught stealing apples.

Sam came straight to the point. "I understand you have shown some interest in my niece, Florence."

"Where did you hear that?"

"From the Doc. And the Sheriff, and Pete Mansfield, and Charlie and Amos, and just about anybody in Dickinson who can see."

"Was it that obvious?"

"Ain't nothing small enough to not be obvious in a community this size."

Jesse took off his hat and wiped at his brow. "I don't know how to say this, but I am very interested in your niece." Jesse had a terribly sheepish look on his face as if he were confessing sins to a priest. "We talked a little bit about this last week, Sam. Florence wanted some time to think about it. She said there were some things I should know about her before we..." He stopped for a moment, then. "Well, she said she had to sort of prepare me for something. I know it ain't been but a short time, but I would like to ask Florence to marry me, and I know she ain't got any parents to ask her hand."

"Did you know she was married once?"

"No, I didn't. But if that's what she wanted to prepare me for, that makes no difference."

"Her husband was a captain in the cavalry. He was killed in an Indian skirmish in Montana about a year ago."

"I'm sorry to hear that." He nodded. "I'm sure she was a fine wife for him, and I believe she would be a fine wife for me."

"She knows about you losing your family?

Jesse nodded. "I told her."

At that moment, Florence appeared in the hotel doorway, wearing a pretty pink dress and a warm smile.

Sam saw the radiance dance within Jesse's face when he spotted her.

Jesse climbed the few steps and stood across from her. "Sam just told me about you losing your husband. I'm very sorry for that."

"Is that all he told you?"

Jesse didn't know what she meant.

Florence turned to the door and beckoned with her hand. "Come," she said. In seconds a little girl quickly ran to her side, grabbed her by the leg and held tight, and moments later a young lad joined her.

Jesse's eyes widened.

"This is Anna and Jacob. Children, this is Mr. Harker."

Jesse stepped forward and offered his hand to Jacob. "Mighty strong handshake you have, son. How old are you?"

"Nine."

"Can you ride a horse?"

"Yessir."

"Can you tend cattle?"

"I can learn, sir."

Jesse looked at the young girl. "I don't ride horses," she volunteered. "And I'm afraid of cows."

"What do you like?" asked Jesse.

"Little chickens and little ducks."

"Nothing wrong with that."

Little Anna stared up at him with huge, brown eyes. Both children were blondes, even though their mother was a brunette.

Then very calmly Anna blurted out, "Are you going to be my new daddy?"

Florence gave Jesse a curious look. "I told you there were

some things you should know about me, so I sent for the children this past week. I hope you're not disappointed."

Anna looked up at her mother. "Is he going to be our new daddy?"

It was all Jesse could do to hold back tears of joy. "What do you say we all go for a ride in the buckboard?" He had barely made the offer when both kids ran for the wagon and clambered in the back.

"Florence?" Jesse said as he offered a hand.

Once they were all in the wagon, little Anna inquired, "Where are we going?"

"Oh, around town," said Jesse. "Maybe stop off at Charlie's and see if he has an extra horse for sale, then run down to Mrs. Bunker's house and see if she has some extra chickens."

"And ducks?" asked Anna.

"Oh, I think she might have some ducks, too. And then to-morrow, maybe we could all ride down to the ranch and spend the day, maybe even have a picnic. That is, if it's okay with your mom."

Both jumped up and down with excitement and implored Florence to agree.

Florence straightened smartly in the seat and turned to the children in the back. With a huge, warm smile she answered, "It's okay with mom."

Jesse snapped the reins, turned the wagon around and headed right down the middle of the street. About half way through town, Pete Mansfield came from the other direction, and as they passed the two exchanged greetings.

By the time Pete Mansfield reached the hotel, Doc Wielding, Sheriff Halverson and Amos Blomberg were standing on the steps with Sam Beaker.

Pete drew to a halt and looked over at the men. "It's lookin' good, ain't it?"

Everybody was grinning from ear to ear. "It sure is," said Sam."

Since that day when Pete found Jesse at the gravesite of his family in the middle of a rain storm, they all knew they had to do something to bring Jesse back into the world of the living. Sam knew Jesse better than anybody in town, and he knew his niece just as well. He had a strong suspicion that she and the children and Jesse would all be good for each other, and so far he was right.

"Yessir," said Sam. "Ain't we a bunch of matchmakers."

They all nodded in agreement.

"It's a bit early, but what say we all go down to the saloon and celebrate?"

Pete Mansfield tied the reins of his horses to a post and joined them. "When do you suppose the event will be?"

"I'd bet in about a week," said Doc Wielding.

Sheriff Halverson laughed. "I ain't gonna take that bet."

They were still laughing when they entered the saloon.

Old Strike

When John walked over the last hill he marveled at the view below and knew at once why they called it the Greenwood Agency. The set of buildings was spaced nicely in and among a thick bunch of cottonwoods, oak and maple. Beyond he could see the tips of many teepees strung out along the Missouri River.

It almost took his breath away as he set his gaze upon the huge expanse of flatland below, some of the acreage planted with wheat and corn. He had made the fifty-mile trek on foot from Yankton over the past two days, walking over a virtually treeless plain of rolling hills. Here and there along the way, trees lined the Missouri banks, but the view now from this small bluff was absolutely refreshing. His view stretched to the far side of the river, where the Nebraska breaks ran sharply down to the water. On this side, an abundance of ducks and geese and seagulls floated lazily along the water's edge.

He sat down to rest for a few moments, and as he did so a loud squawk startled him. Seconds later a blue crane cranked by just yards away from his head, then circled below and landed in some reeds along the bank.

He heard distant voices for a moment, and then far ahead he saw a boat shove off from shore. Two men were headed across to the Nebraska side for one reason or other. He watched them for some time, then picked up his bundle of belongings once again. He slung the strap over his shoulder and trudged downward using the diamond willow walking stick, which an uncle had given him before he left. It was an ornate piece of twisted wood, carved nicely and stained with a reddish oil. A copper ring circled the bottom to prevent the wooden tip from splintering, and another copper ring trimmed the top of the stick.

John Dvoracek had immigrated to this vast land of opportunity from Czechoslovakia like so many other Bohemians before him. That was two years ago in 1870. He had farmed with relatives since his arrival, and when the position to work at the Greenwood Agency was presented to him, he jumped at the offer. The pay wasn't great, but the job granted board and room, which made up for it, and he was guaranteed an experience that would present challenge after challenge working among the Indians, or so the Circuit Judge had said. After John accepted the position, he discovered he was the only one who had applied for the job, but that made no difference. He was looking at this job not only as a challenge, but also a welcome change from plowing behind a span of workhorses in the hot Dakota Territory sun. John was only twenty-one years old, but as young as he was, he decided he did not want to spend the rest of his life farming.

He had been given a book in which he was to study the culture of the Yankton Sioux Indians, but he himself was not a good reader of English, although he thought that after two years in this country he had a fairly good command of the spoken language. So far he had read very little of the book and decided it would be easier to learn about the Sioux as he went along.

Ben Friederich saw John coming and figured out immediately who he was. He had received information this man would be arriving soon, and he was told that although John Dvoracek was small in stature, barely over five feet, he was spunky and strong and had excellent carpenter skills.

John saw Ben Friederich standing outside the livery building and knew immediately who he was. He had been informed Ben was a six-footer, a veteran of three years at the agency already, and the man in charge.

"I'm guessing you're Mr. Dvoracek," said Ben in the Czech language as he stuck out a hand.

"Yessir, and you are Ben Friederich?" answered John in Czech.

"I am. I hope you didn't wear out your souls getting here."

John lifted one shoe and looked at the bottom of it. "Not yet."

"You don't own a horse?" Ben asked.

"No."

"Know how to ride one?"

John looked at the horses in the corral next to the livery, which were cow ponies. The only horseback riding John had done was on a Shire plow horse that weighed 1600 pounds and had a back broad enough to challenge the seat of any rider. He had never been in a saddle before.

"Well, I have ridden," John finally confessed, his eyes still on the horses. "But nothing that small."

Ben laughed out loud, and then said. "What do you know about farm machinery?"

John was slow to answer and somewhat perturbed, since he thought he was getting out of the farming business. "Well, I know a little bit about farming."

"How would you like to help the Indians learn how to plow and plant?"

John frowned, looked back at the corral. "I think I'd rather ride horse."

Ben laughed again. "Know anything about carpentry?"

John's bright blue eyes sparkled. "Yes, I do. I helped build many a barn and shed back in Bratislava."

"Did you ever build a church?"

"Nope, I haven't. Don't know as I ever met anyone who did."

"Neither have I," said Ben as he motioned for John to follow him. The two walked a hundred yards down a dirt road to an area where several trees had been cleared. "We're going to build a church right there."

John looked the area over, then turned around and saw the

Missouri a few hundred yards away. "Sure is a nice view."

"Picked the spot out myself. You hungry?"

"Famished," said John.

"So am I. I'll show you your quarters. By the time you're washed up, Helga should have supper on."

As they walked down the dirt road, John saw a few Indians here and there, most just lounging in the shade. As they neared the building, which housed the workers at the agency, they passed an older fellow sitting on the porch bench outside the building.

"That's Old Strike. He knows more about this country than you and I will ever learn in our life time."

John got a good look at the old man. His face was the color of the leather on John's shoes, with wrinkles so deep that his skin looked like it was cracked. He wore a blue denim shirt with buckskin pants and moccasins, and on his head sat a fur cap that looked like it was made from muskrat. As John and Ben entered the housing unit, Old Strike's eyes seemed to be focused on the walking stick John was carrying.

Inside, a long table occupied the center of a fair-sized room, and off to the right was the kitchen area where Helga, a good-looking young lady, was busy cooking.

Ben looked at Helga. "Meet John Dvoracek, our new carpenter."

Helga was about the same height as John, a little on the stout side, but with a friendly, round Czech face. As she wiped her hands in her apron she gave John a slight curtsey. "Pleased to meet you. I'm Helga Friederich."

John looked at Ben. "I didn't know you had a wife."

"Helga's not my wife, she's my sister."

John smiled and abruptly offered his hand. He didn't know if a handshake was protocol with a woman, but he thought it would be a pleasant experience just to touch her skin, and it was.

Ben showed John to his room, which was small, and at the evening meal he met three other Czech workers, Emil Kopal, Frank

Matushka and Ernest Blezek, all assigned to various duties at the agency. Helga kept the housing quarters in order, cooked, did laundry and just about anything else required of a woman, which included keeping the books.

Over the next few days, John made the rounds of the agency. He became better acquainted with the other three workers, and after having been paraded through the grounds where the Indians camped, he took a better interest in the book he had received about the Yankton Sioux culture.

Ben provided him with a horse and saddle, and John took it upon himself to simply ride about the community and familiarize himself with the land. One afternoon he trotted the animal along a few teepees, and as he did so, Old Strike, the Indian he had seen a few days before, came out of his tent and watched as John rode by.

Fifteen minutes later, when John trotted by the same tent, Old Strike was still at his place and once again looked John over very carefully. The old Indian held up a hand and John reined in his horse.

Old Strike positioned his hands one above another and slapped the top of one hand with the palm of the other several times, then said to John in clear English, "Your ass takes much pounding. That is not good."

John understood the man and was mildly surprised at his language. At that moment two Indians riding bareback came from the other direction, trotting their animals much like John had been doing, but their butts were not bouncing up and down.

Old Strike placed one hand over the other and rubbed them gently together. "Smooth," he said to John. "No pounding ass. Someday maybe you ride like Indian."

John smiled, removed his hat and wiped the sweat away from his brow. He could see Old Strike also was sweating about the temples, but the old man did not bother to remove his hat to wipe away the perspiration.

"My name is John Dvoracek."

"You carpenter," said the Indian.

"Yes, I am. What do you do?" asked John.

Old Strike struck a gaze like a stone, dumbfounded with the question. Finally, he said. "I am chief." He made a sweeping motion with his hands towards the teepees. "I govern."

It took John a moment to understand what the word *govern* meant, and then it came clear to him that the Chief basically ran the camp. His duties were probably restricted to that, since John assumed the Indians were no longer on the warpath. John tipped his hat as a friendly gesture when he left, rode back to the livery stable and put up his horse before heading for his quarters.

Over the next few days, the men began the initial excavation on the new church. Supplies had been ordered from Yankton, but the foundation needed to be done, so John, Emil and Ernie laid out the measurements, and with a flat blade pulled behind a pair of mules, they began to level the ground in preparation for the cement block foundation. John had done masonry work before, so he was put in charge of that portion of the project. The days were hot and long, and every morning, noon and afternoon Helga showed up with coffee and sandwiches. A tall milk pail filled with cold water in the morning was almost empty at the end of every day. It seemed that every fifteen minutes the men were drinking a few ladles of water just to keep from dehydrating.

Every day about mid morning, Old Strike would show up and place himself on a stump where he would spend a good portion of the day watching as the men labored away at the tedious work. On extremely hot days, he left early, but his usual position was now referred to as *Old Strike's private stump.*

Sometimes other Indian adults or children would stop and watch the men work, but if Old Strike ever showed up, anyone who was sitting on the stump relinquished it to the old Indian Chief. Without a doubt, being Chief had definite benefits.

The Indians would usually talk among themselves, and John assumed their chatter probably centered on the methodology of building the structure. On one occasion they all burst out in laughter, and Ernie Blezek, who overheard the Indians and understood some Sioux, was also laughing.

"What's so funny?" asked John.

"It seems the tribal members have a nickname for you."

John was amused. "What is it?"

Ernie pulled a face. "I'm not sure of the translation, but something like John Hard Ass. Does that make sense to you?"

John knew immediately what the Indians meant, and when he looked over at Old Strike, the old Indian slapped his hands together. The small crowd of Indians laughed and laughed over John's new Indian name.

It seemed the Indians had their own names for the various white men who worked at the agency. Ben was known as *Ben Long Stick*, because of his thin frame and height. Ernie was known as *Short Walker*, since when he walked he seemed to take tiny steps. Frank Matushka usually tended cattle, so he was known as the *Lone Rider*. Ernie's name was *Man Who Whistles* and Helga was known as *Pretty Face*.

The nickname *John Pounding Ass* did not bother John, but it did force him to make a concerted effort in the next several days to practice riding. He took pointers from anyone that would give them to him, but Frank was the best source, since he spent almost every day in the saddle.

Within a week, the cement blocks for the foundation of the church were squared up and the men began setting the floor joists in place. Inside of two days, they ran out of lumber, and the work came to a halt. It would not continue until the next load of supplies arrived from Yankton, so John took it upon himself to ride more and more each day and spent several hours riding herd with Frank. In due time, John was feeling fairly confident in his ability to ride, and one evening on the way back to the agency he made a point to purposely ride past Old Strike's tent. The old Chief was sitting on a blanket against a tree carving on a stick when John rode past. John made an extreme effort to keep his horse in a trot and show off his new ability, and when he looked back, he saw that the old Indian gave a favorable nod.

A couple days passed and John and Ben were talking with each other. "Doesn't Old Strike ever take off that muskrat hat?" John inquired.

"I've never seen him without it," said Ben. "It's kind of a trademark with him."

John had asked all the men and Helga the same question, but nobody had an answer. Thinking that the hat might have had some religious significance, John checked in his Sioux book of culture. Eagle feathers signified signs of bravery or great deeds, and full headdresses signified positions of prestige, like chiefs or shamans, but the muskrat hat played no role anywhere in the book. Most clothing was made from deer or buffalo or elk, but rarely was a full garment made of muskrat, so none of the men understood the significance of the hat. In winter, wearing such a fur hat made sense, but in summer it seemed the old man should be satisfied with a simple headband, like so many other members of the tribe wore.

The next day two wagonloads of lumber arrived from the Yankton millwork and the men set to work again, positioning planks for the floor and building the framework of the superstructure. John had a rough blueprint to follow, but modifications were imminent, especially when Pastor Pavel arrived in his buggy to survey the progress.

"Praise the Lord," the pastor seemed to begin with each suggested change, and there were many. Most recommendations were minor, but the clergyman insisted that an office in back of the altar and an extra room for Sunday school children was an absolute necessity. When it was pointed out there were very few whites in the area with children, Pastor Pavel raised an eyebrow.

"This is God's church, which is meant for all races red and white."

John's mind reflected on what he had read in the Sioux culture book. "Do you think you can entice the Indians into this church?" he asked.

"Of course," replied the frumpy man.

John felt an inward urge to laugh. The Sioux, from what he knew, had their own spirituality, which centered on the elements of the earth. Earth and sky were an inherent part of their religion as well as a great respect for the outdoors. John told the pastor that the white man had not been able to bring the Indians into man-made structures to live, so why would he think he could entice them to pray in a building made of mortar and wood?

Questions of that nature did not sit well with Pastor Pavel, and his look of disgust at such inquires was enough to kill, however, as a man of God, a killing look was as close as he ever came to the full use of word.

The foundation of the Church was already laid, and if the men shortened the main floor any to make an office space and a schoolroom, three rows of pews would have to be removed. Faced with the possibility of cutting his congregation short by perhaps eighteen people, Pastor Pavel finally relented.

Disgruntled, the man of the clergy crawled back in his buggy and left for Yankton. He was barely out of earshot when all the men said almost in unison, "Praise the Lord."

When Sunday rolled around, everyone took the day off. A short church session was held outside the living quarters in the shade with Ben reading a few words out of the Bible, followed with some common hymns. A few farm families in the area also showed up for the service. They were interested in the progress of the church as well as any new gossip in the community, and late in the afternoon they all headed home.

The next several days were so hot, even the nights refused to cool down. John wished he had prayed for rain on the preceding Sunday, but the thought had not occurred to him at the time. They continued to work in spite of the miserable heat, and now the men were finishing off two full milk pails of water each day. Every evening about dark, John took a dip in the Missouri to cool off, an effort that was good so long as one remained in the water. However, once out of it, the humidity and the mosquitoes did their utmost to make mere existence in the outdoors as miserable as one could imagine. John could not begin to fathom how the Indians tolerated such conditions, and he was amazed that they did not complain near as much as the whites.

The progress on the church was making good strides, and even though it was hot, Old Strike always showed up and always wore the same muskrat hat on his head. The men now made it a point to keep their eye on him, thinking they might on some occasion see him remove the hat and smooth down his hair, but no one ever was witness to the event.

In the several weeks that John had been working at the agency, he had met some of the tribal members and knew many by their names. He had not once inquired, however, if any of the Sioux people knew why Old Strike never removed his hat, since it was not etiquette to inquire of another person's idiosyncrasies, and this certainly was an idiosyncrasy. The men even made bets among themselves, which would first see the old chief with his muskrat hat removed, and though all had a quarter bet on the challenge, no one in the ensuing days collected.

John had become fairly well acquainted with Old Strike and often had conversations with him, as brief as they were. Since there appeared to be a growing friendship between the two, John inquired of Ben and Helga whether it was permissible to invite Old Strike in for a white man's meal. No one had any objections, and so John invited the chief to join them one evening at supper.

Old Strike considered it a complement to be invited into the white man's dwelling, and he showed up on the night he was invited, though nearly an hour late. When everyone sat down at the table, Old Strike was given a place and waited for instructions how to proceed. He knew about the utensils the white people utilized, but he had never used them before.

Before they ate, Ben asked that they say a prayer, and when Old Strike agreed to hear the offering, it struck John that the man was still wearing his muskrat hat.

"It is a custom to remove one's hat at the table," said John to the chief.

Old Strike stared at John.

"Chief," repeated John. "It is the white man's way of giving thanks. We remove our hats at the table."

The chief made a face of stone as he looked about him and observed the faces staring back at him, all anxiously waiting for his response.

John asked a third time. "Can you remove your hat while we..."

Before John could finish, the Chief jumped up and pulled a knife from his belt. He stood for several seconds, his hand tight about the handle, his hand shaking violently. He kept his eyes on John for the longest time and then saw the fear in all the faces around the table.

He slowly put his knife away, left the house and walked back to his camp. John was embarrassed, even felt hurt that he had asked the man to remove his cap. Obviously he had insulted the man, but he didn't know why.

The meal that night was eaten in complete silence, and for the rest of the night, John sat next to a lamp in his room and read through the book of Sioux culture, searching for a paragraph that might explain the anger he had aroused in Old Strike.

Three days passed, and although the men worked every day on the church and were beginning to see the walls take shape, not once did Old Strike show up to assess the progress. No one felt more badly than John did, since he was the one who had asked Old Strike to remove his hat at the table. No one chided him, stating that it was such common practice, and at the time they thought nothing of it. Most were thinking that with the initial inquiry to remove the hat, the least they would have to do was pay up the quarter bet.

The following Sunday, the community held its church service inside the new structure even though the roof was not yet in place. That afternoon John asked Helga if she would care to take a walk with him, to which she consented. John took along his diamond willow walking stick and Helga packed a small lunch, and off they went. The two circumvented the Indian camp by walking over the bluff, and in due time they located a shady setting near the mouth of a creek that fed into the Missouri.

They had just spread out a blanket and sat down when a bunch of little Indian boys and girls ran past them and headed for the banks of the creek. In no time, the half dozen kids had shucked most of their clothes and were frolicking in the water.

John had intended to find a private spot, but Helga told him that this was a common water hole for the children. Although the kids were noisy, neither of the two minded, and in fact the screaming and laughter was a welcome sound in the heat of the day.

A half-hour had passed when suddenly the laughter of the kids changed somewhat. Helga was the first to hear the pleas.

"Someone needs help!" she said as she jumped to her feet. John was up and running in the direction of the kids, and when he reached the bank, the youngsters were hollering and pointing out into the Missouri. One of the kids had gone out too far and was caught in the main current.

John saw a head bob, and then the child disappeared under the water. He shucked his shoes and tore his trousers off as quickly as he could and jumped into the water. He swam quickly to where he had last seen the child go under, but when he reached the spot the child was not to be seen.

"There! There!" he heard Helga shout as he watched her point. In just a few seconds he reached the little girl, and with powerful strokes he pulled her back to shore. She was unconscious and the only thing John knew about reviving a victim was to roll the person over a log. He carried her quickly to a downed tree and placed her belly down across the log. With everyone looking on, their faces wrought with fear, John rolled the limp body back and forth for what seemed like minutes.

Finally the young girl spewed water out of her mouth, and after a short coughing spell she began crying more out of fear than anything else. Helga took the little girl in her arms and rocked her, consoling her with some Sioux words.

John put his clothes back on, and then carried the little girl back to camp. Several of the other children ran on ahead to deliver the news of the near tragedy, and when John walked into the village, several tribal members were there to greet him, among them the mother of the child.

She was ever so grateful, and though she gave her thanks in the Sioux language, John did not understand her words, but he understood her meaning.

The next day began with gray, rolling clouds on the horizon, and shortly after breakfast, a welcome, steady rain was coming down. Since the men could not work on the church, John threw on a slicker and ran to the livery, where he began oiling down the saddle he usually used.

While he was working on the saddle, Old Strike entered the building. The man had a pancho-like affair about his neck to protect himself from the rain and sat on a sawhorse opposite John for the longest time, simply looking at him. John could see the concerned look in the man's face.

Finally he spoke. "You save Little Wolf from the river."

John was silent for a moment. "Yes."

"Little Wolf is my granddaughter."

John quit rubbing in the oil. "I did not know."

"Old Strike is grateful. The Great Spirit was good to me yesterday. I come today to apologize."

"For what?" asked John.

"I pulled knife on you. I am sorry."

John felt humble. "It was our custom to remove hats at the table. If that was not your custom, I too am sorry for asking."

The old chief nodded, then reached up an old hand and slowly removed his muskrat cap. John stared incredulously at the man's head. A huge hunk of hair above his forehead was gone, the scared skin now hardened and red.

"Many years ago," he began, "I was in battle against the Arikara tribe. I fell in battle and was scalped by the enemy and left for dead. My people found me and gave me life once again." He pointed to his head. "I must live with this. It is not easy for me. I hope you understand."

John could not be more humble. "I do understand," he said as he offered a hand to the old man. "It shall be our secret forever."

The Chief held John's hand for the longest time. He put his muskrat hat back on and then removed a necklace from around his neck and placed it over John's head. "My father gave me this when I was a little boy."

He nodded his head as a gesture of forgiveness, then walked out into the rain and headed back to his teepee.

That night, though the rain was still coming down, John walked to the Chief's tent and left his diamond willow walking stick outside on the ground. He knew Old Strike had observed the curiously twisted wood with the red stain and copper rings, and he also knew the man admired it.

The church work continued for the next several weeks, and by September it was ready for use.

Each day during those several weeks, Old Strike had showed up to watch the progress, and each day he had appeared with his prized, diamond willow walking stick.

Author's note: My Great Grandfather, John Dvoracek, worked at the Greenwood Agency for several years in the 1870's before he took up farming in the area of Tabor, South Dakota. Although most of this story is fictionalized, my Great Grandfather wrote in his memoirs that the incident with the knife by Old Strike actually took place, and that after the incident, the two still remained good friends. Great Grandfather helped build one of the churches at the Greenwood Agency and also ended up marrying the Friederich girl.

Another piece of related history enters here. When Lewis and Clark landed at the original Yankton Sioux camp in 1804 during their expedition, a son was born to a Yankton chief at the time. Lewis wrapped the newborn in an American flag and proclaimed him an American citizen, and prophesized that the son would grow up to be a great chief. That young boy eventually was known as Struck by the Ree, a prominent Chief among the Yankton Sioux, and went by the name in his later years as Old Strike.

———— ♦ ————

Private Buckley

When First Sergeant Gunnerson heard the hoof beats of the oncoming horses, he left the confines of the storage house and walked out onto the loading platform just in time to see the soldiers coming through the gates of the fort. He had wiped the sweat from his brow and already put his handkerchief away by the time the riders brought their mounts to a halt.

"Dismount, find yourselves some water," the officer commanded to the four soldiers with him.

"Hello, Lieutenant," said the First Sergeant in greeting. "Thought you was supposed to have eight men."

"We did when we left," the Lieutenant said as he took off his gauntlets and wiped his forehead. "Four deserted last night. Wasn't no sense wasting our time trying to run down that low-down lot. Five of us chasing four of them was hardly a posse under any circumstances."

The Sergeant shook his head. "I know duty's pretty tough at Fort Fetterman."

The Lieutenant laughed. "That's an understatement. Hotter'n hell in summer, colder'n hell in winter, no hog house for the men within fifty miles and nothing to do. The boredom alone can kill you. If I was just an officer, I'd have joined them. But unfortunately I'm an officer and a gentleman."

The Sergeant smiled.

The Lieutenant looked around. "I see everybody's about gone."

124

"Yep," said the Sergeant. "The Colonel and the last troop left for Laramie couple days ago. Just me and a handful of boys left. Soon's we load up your two wagons, we're out of here." He glanced around the Fort Caspar grounds. "I'm going to miss her. She's been my home for three years."

The Lieutenant focused on the stable where he could see only a few horses. "I was supposed to have six more soldiers as escorts back to Fort Fetterman. Where are they?"

"Coming up from Medicine Bow. They should have been here already. Don't know what's keeping them. Sergeant O'Mallery and five of his boys. You'll be happy to have him on your side. He's got twenty years of service and shot more Indians than you ever seen."

"Oh, I've seen a few," answered the Lieutenant. "Even shot at a few. Don't know as I ever hit one."

A rattling wagon drawn by a pair of matched grays entered the fort.

"That's Old Jake Littlefield," said the Sergeant. Sitting on the front seat alongside him was a soldier, his uniform dirty and torn. When the wagon stopped, Jake stepped from the seat and pulled a tarp back. Five soldiers lay dead, among them Sergeant O'Mallery.

"Jesus!" said the Lieutenant.

"Found em' this mornin' bout twenty miles south," said Jake. "All dead cep'n for this young private here."

"What happened, soldier?" asked the Sergeant.

"Indians attacked our camp at dawn. Took all our horses and guns. I just crawled out of my bedroll when something struck me on the head. That's all I know."

The sergeant checked over the bodies of the dead soldiers. All had multiple wounds, three had been scalped. "You're damn lucky," said the sergeant to the soldier. "What's your name?"

"Private Everett Buckley, from Nebraska, sir. My papers say I'm supposed to be assigned to the 3rd cavalry."

The Sergeant nodded. "This is Lieutenant Hartley, Company C from Fort Fetterman. He's your new assignment."

Private Buckley stuck out a hand. "Pleased to know you, sir."

The Lieutenant expected a salute, but overlooked the unsoldierly conduct and shook Buckley's hand.

"Been in the military long?" asked the Lieutenant.

"No, sir. This is my first duty."

"It's been a tough one. You feeling okay?"

"Yes, sir."

"Get yourself cleaned up and find something to eat."

"Yes, sir."

First Sergeant Gunnerson summoned one of his men and sent the two off to the enlisted men's quarters. He turned to Jake. "Was it Sioux what done it?"

"No doubt about it," said Jake. "They was Sioux arrows. Probably some of Red Cloud's band. Thought we was making a treaty with him."

The Lieutenant made a face. "It's in the makings, but in the meanwhile Red Cloud keeps reminding us this is his land." He gripped the side of the wagon and stared down at the dead soldiers. Let's get a detail together and put these men to rest."

"Yes, sir," said the Sergeant.

By nightfall they had buried the five men at the end of the grounds. There was no one to play taps and no chaplain to offer a prayer. First Sergeant Gunnerson read a few Bible verses and delivered some personal words for the slain men, hopeful that his short eulogy would suffice in sending the men off into the next world.

Afterward the men skipped protocol and went to the Caspar Hotel where they ordered a good, hearty meal, paid for by the U.S. Cavalry.

By sunup the next day, as soldiers were loading the remaining supplies in the wagons, Sheriff Glen Buford rode in, a big and burly man like the First Sergeant. He stepped down from his horse. "Mornin' Sarge. I see you boys are about to pull out."

"Yep. Another hour or so and we should be packed."

"You fellas plan on following up on that Indian fight yesterday?"

"Nope," answered the Sergeant. "Ain't got nobody to spare. This morning we dispatched one of our soldiers to Medicine Bow with a report. Could hardly afford to send him, but the Lieutenant said it was the least we could do for the five dead men."

"Well, I hope he gets through. Folks around here get a bit jumpy when that sort of thing happens, especially this close to town."

Lieutenant Hartley came across the grounds from the headquarters building. The Sergeant introduced him to Sheriff Buford.

"I understand you boys are headed back to Fort Laramie," said the Sheriff.

"One wagon's headed that way," answered the Lieutenant. "Yesterday we decided Sergeant Gunnerson would accompany me back to Fort Fetterman. We'll take a five soldier escort, the rest will go with the other wagon."

The Sheriff nodded, frowned. "One wagon south of the Platte, two on the north side. Cuttin' it kind of thin, ain't you?"

"We don't have much choice," said the Lieutenant as he pointed to the graves at the far end of the fort.

"Yeah, we were sorry to hear about that." The Sheriff paused and spit out some brown goo on the ground. "Well, the reason I asked is there was an attempted train robbery in Cheyenne a few days back. Couple railroad men got killed, and we got reason to believe the outlaws that did it might be headed this way."

"Who are they?" asked the Lieutenant.

"We don't know for sure. Some say it's the Lowrys from up north, others think it's the Hale brothers from the Medicine Bow area. About all we know for sure is there's at least five of them, and well armed."

"We'll keep our eyes peeled," said the Sergeant.

"And then one other problem. One of my deputies thinks he seen a fella by the name of Kid Barns at the Horseshoe Inn. Some sort of gunfighter. There's a warrant for his arrest, but I don't even have a poster on him. Some say he's one hell of a good shot with a pistol and rifle. As good as or better than Bill Cody."

They had all heard of Buffalo Bill Cody.

"How we supposed to recognize him if you don't have a poster on him?" asked the Sergeant.

"He rides a big black, sixteen hands or better. He's outrun many a posse, and I doubt he would give him up. That black horse is a roving landmark if you ask me."

The Sheriff spat another gob. "You know, it's quiet around here for months at a time, then suddenly we got this Indian massacre and a bunch of train robbers, and now this Kid Barns gunslinger. Whole town's getting riled up. I got a posse waiting for me back at the stable and don't even know which way to go."

He heaved his big frame into the saddle. "You see anything suspicious, be on guard." He touched his hat. "Good knowing you, Sergeant Gunnerson."

Inside of an hour, the wagons were loaded and tarps flung over the top for protection.

"Private Buckley," said the Lieutenant. "You know how to drive one of these rigs?"

"Yes, sir. But I prefer the saddle."

The Lieutenant eyed the young private. He expected him to simply accept the assigned duty. "All right. Pick out a horse. Sergeant Gunnerson, get him a sidearm and a carbine and assemble the men. We're moving out."

"Yes, sir!" snapped the Sergeant.

By ten o'clock they reached the Platte Bridge, where one wagon with a driver and three escorts followed the tracks of the Oregon Trail, which led back to Fort Laramie.

"See you boys in a week," Sergeant Gunnerson hollered after them. He headed his wagon up onto the Platte Bridge, followed by Private Riley driving the second rig. Private Buckley rode guard along with three other soldiers. Two additional horses, both saddled, were tethered to the last wagon.

Anyone passing over the bridge had to pay a toll, but the keeper waved the military men through like he had done so many times before. As the wagons reached the north side of the river and headed back east, Sergeant Gunnerson took one last look at the fort, and within another mile it was out of sight.

They traveled for the better part of the day without incident. Neither the Lieutenant nor the Sergeant expected any trouble, at least not from Indians. If they by chance came under attack, the two wagons were to line up alongside each other leaving just enough space between to serve as a barricade on both sides. They were to tether the two horses in between at the rear forming a live breastwork out of the animals. The wagons contained enough extra ammunition to stand off a formidable force if need be, which seemed reassuring to the men.

Though all the enlisted men had single shot carbines, the Lieutenant carried a Henry repeating rifle in his scabbard. It was not military issue, but anyone who could afford such a rifle, officer or otherwise could have one. Earning fifteen dollars a month rarely provided enlisted men with this kind of luxury.

At all times during the trip, the Lieutenant rode ahead, and one soldier flanked each side of the two wagons as lookouts. Private Buckley took his turn when it came up. This was new country for him, wide open and barren for the most part. The south wind was strong and hot and blew the grass in gentle waves, giving this vastness a sense of serenity that all the men seemed to enjoy.

On occasion when Private Buckley was as much as a half-mile from the two-wagon train, he could hear the Sergeant singing.

When evening came they had covered close to twenty miles, almost half the distance to Fort Fetterman. Though their trail took them through some wooded areas, they chose to make camp on high, open ground from where they could easily see in all directions. For security, the Lieutenant had two guards posted during the night, and Sergeant Gunnerson formed a corral between the two wagons where the horses were kept. The meal was beans, bacon and biscuits, a good hot meal.

Shortly after sunup, the horses were hitched to the wagons, and the small troop was on its way. With a little luck, they were sure they could reach Fort Fetterman by nightfall.

In the early afternoon, Private Buckley was guarding the left flank of the wagons no more than 300 yards distant. They had just entered some small rising hills, but as far ahead as he could see, the country was open, nothing in sight.

He glanced toward the teams of horses in a draw below. The Lieutenant was out front, the two other soldiers trailing behind. On a rise across from him, Private Buckley could see the soldier whom everyone called Shorty. They happened to be looking at each other at the same time and were exchanging a wave of the hand, when suddenly Shorty fell from his horse flat on the ground. Moments later Buckley heard the muffled report of a rifle.

Buckley spurred his horse toward the wagons. The Lieutenant had also heard the shot and was riding full force back to his men. Then all hell broke loose. On the rise beyond where Shorty fell, three riders appeared. Buckley saw the smoke from their rifles, and in seconds one horse from each of the wagons fell, both struck by the bullets of the attackers.

Shots resounded from near Buckley now, and as he turned in the saddle he saw two more riders coming in fast from behind him. He spurred his mount even more, and while at a full gallop his horse took a bullet and collapsed underneath him. Buckley flew off the back of the animal, rolled and came up running for the shelter of the wagons.

More shots rang out. He heard Sergeant Gunnerson holler, and saw him fall from the wagon seat. Riley, the driver of the second rig slumped over. The Lieutenant was shouting commands, his pistol drawn, his horse bucking. A shot echoed and spun the Lieutenant out of his saddle. He hit the ground and grabbed his shoulder as he ran for the wagons.

Private Buckley saw the stock of the Henry rifle sticking out of the scabbard. He ran for the Lieutenant's horse, bullets thumping all around him, and yanked the Henry rifle from its place. With more bullets tearing up the ground around him, he raced back to the wagons. The two soldiers who had been riding behind were both down, their horses racing off in different directions.

The Sergeant had taken a shot in the side, but he staggered to his feet and shoved another round into his carbine. Blood stained the Lieutenant's right shoulder. He had switched his pistol to his left hand and was firing rapidly, but his aim was not good. Bullets rained in from every direction.

"Jesus!" screamed the Lieutenant. "They've got repeaters!"

The riders, good horsemen, kept coming, three from the south, two from behind, another ahead of them now, their guns blazing.

Private Buckley raised the Henry rifle, coolly took aim and squeezed off a shot. One of the riders dropped from the saddle. He took careful aim again and another man dropped.

Bullets tore into the wagon box next to him. He whirled around and fired two rounds. Both men screamed out as they flew from their saddles.

"By Jesus!" he heard the Lieutenant holler out. "This kid can shoot!"

From ahead of the horses, another rider came in fast, his six shooter firing round after round. Young Private Buckley pulled the Army colt from his holster, and as the rider came into his sights, he fired and saw the bullet strike the man in the arm flipping his pistol away. As the man rode past, young Buckley fired another round that caught him in the chest, throwing him off his mount.

Five of the six attackers were now down. The one remaining rider abruptly turned his horse and headed up the hillside, scrambling for shelter on the other side. Private Buckley rested the Henry rifle on top of the wagon box, and just as the horseman reached the summit, Buckley fired a final round. The man's hands flailed in the air and he tumbled backwards off his horse, dead before he hit the ground.

"Good God," said the Sergeant. "That was 300 yards!"

It was now ever so quiet as the three men looked over the battlefield. None of the six attackers was moving. Riley and the two soldiers riding rear guard were dead. Private Buckley rode the Lieutenant's horse up the hill where Shorty had been shot. He, too, was dead.

The Lieutenant had taken a clean shot through the shoulder. He was sore, but at least he hadn't broken a bone. The bullet that had struck the Sergeant was a glancing shot to his hip, but he managed to stop the bleeding. Both of these men would survive their wounds.

Inside of an hour, Private Buckley had unharnessed the two dead horses from the wagons and dragged them away using a lariat. The Lieutenant helped Buckley as best he could to hitch up two saddle horses in their place. Then, one by one, Private Buckley brought each of the men he had killed back to the wagon and laid them in a row next to the trail. He gathered their horses and tied them to the back end of the second rig.

With the four dead soldiers in the wagon bed, Lieutenant Hartley, the Sergeant and Private Buckley stood silently for some time, once again looking over the battle ground about them.

"Ain't never seen a soldier what could shoot like you, son," said the Sergeant.

Private Buckley said nothing, stared down at his feet.

"You ain't Private Buckley, are you?" asked the Sergeant

"No, sir. I ain't. My name's William Barnstuble."

"Kid Barns," said the Lieutenant. "What happened to the real Private Buckley?"

"I found him dead with the rest of the soldiers. I buried him, took his clothes and his identity. It seemed like a good idea at the time."

"What you running from?" asked the Sergeant.

"About a year ago I killed a couple men who were cheating me at cards. And since then I killed a couple bounty hunters. Every place I go, the law's after me. I got tired of running, and taking

Private Buckley's identity seemed like a good way out of my predicament."

He looked around and motioned with his hands. "And now that this has happened..." He stopped, shrugged his shoulders. "Besides, it wouldn't be fair to Buckley's family, whoever they are."

The Lieutenant and Sergeant were at a loss. An inquiry on the attempted holdup would be made, questions would be raised, someone would make a report and the young man's true identity would come to light.

The young man, William Barnstuble, examined the dead holdup men. He picked a man about his size, removed his clothes and put them on. From another he selected a hat, and from a third a pistol and holster to his liking.

He removed a sturdy looking saddle from one of the men's horses and threw it on a tall, stout bay, then cinched up the saddle and secured a Winchester rifle in the scabbard.

"I'll ride ahead to Fort Fetterman and send some help back," he said as he swung into the saddle. "If you should see the Sheriff in Caspar, tell him the Lowry bunch won't be giving anybody any more trouble."

He touched the brim of his hat in a final gesture, turned his horse and rode off at a quick pace in the direction of the fort. Lieutenant Hartley and First Sergeant Gunnerson doubted they would ever see him again.

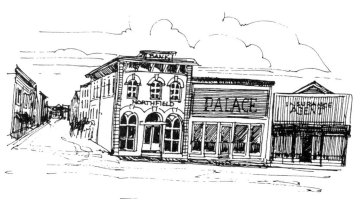

The Reward

It was late in the afternoon on this September day, when Sheriff James Glispin came down the muddy road on his horse, the collar of his rain slicker pulled up tight about his neck to keep out the drizzle and the cold. He rode tall in the saddle, but when he climbed off his sorrel, the top of his hat barely cleared the withers on his 15 hand horse. He was of fair complexion with short brown hair and a bushy mustache. As Sheriff of Watontan County, he was well respected, and though he was normally of quiet demeanor, he was known to stare down the toughest characters with a simple, but determined glance.

The Sheriff removed his hat and wiped at a sultry wet brow, then looked up at Charles Pomeroy. "Anybody come through here today, Mr. Pomeroy?" he asked.

"No, sir," answered Charles. He held back an inward smile when he heard the title. Charles' full name was Charles A. Pomeroy, and almost everybody who knew him addressed him as *Cap*. Charles Pomeroy had known the Sheriff for some time, but it was only of late that he discovered the determination this little man had. Cap wondered what it must be like to be a Sheriff who was so short, that he had to look up at practically everybody. Cap, himself, was a six footer.

The Sheriff looked around. "Your relief men should be here soon. Have you eaten?"

"Nothing all day, sir."

The Sheriff nodded, looked back from where he came. "The

boys up there are kind'a hungry too. And cold. I wish this damn rain would go away. But, I guess it's just as miserable for them boys who robbed the bank."

"Any more word on that?"

"One of them they think was Bill Styles, the other they aren't sure yet. We think this Styles fellow was the same man who checked into the Nicollet House livery in St. Peter. Wherever these boys are from, they cased this area pretty well."

"How many do you think are still on the loose?" asked Cap.

The Sheriff smiled. "God knows. We've had so many reports of four and six, one witness said he seen eight of them. I'm guessing, maybe four or five. But could be, they split up."

"What makes you say that?" asked Cap.

"Last night outside of Lake Crystal, a horse was stolen from a farmer named John Vincent. About midnight, a few miles west of there, little Richie Roberts caught them crossing his picket line. He unloaded two barrels of buckshot and knocked them both off the horse. They ran off in the woods in a hurry, and one of them dropped his hat and didn't stop to pick it up."

"Holy moly," said Cap as he looked across the river to the east. "That ain't too far from here. Those two might have come through here last night."

"That's right," said the Sheriff. Both looked up to see two riders coming their direction down the same muddy road.

"There's your relief for the night. You be back here in the morning?"

"Yessir, you can count me."

"Good boy. We appreciate your help. Are you going directly home?"

"Yessir."

"Well, you keep your eyes peeled along the way. You see anybody suspicious, you go for help first. No need trying to be a hero. Understand me?"

"Yessir."

"Good. You get a good night's rest, Mr. Pomeroy."

Cap climbed on his horse and headed down the road. He had ridden for twenty minutes when he came to the Rockwood farm, his neighbor. As he rode past the drive, he looked down the road toward the farmstead. No one was in sight, and Rockwood's buggy was gone.

Cap didn't think much of it until he came over a rise in the road. George Rockwood was coming his direction in his buckboard. The two pulled up at the same time.

"Howdy, Cap," George greeted. "How are things on the picket line?"

"Nothing today. Nobody's seen anything. What are you doing out riding in this miserable wet?"

"Looking for my two grays. They ran off some time this morning. Don't know how, I had them tied to the hayrack. I foller'd their tracks west a bit, but it's like a damn slough over there." George spit a big gob of tobacco juice and wiped his mouth with his sleeve. "I'll find em, eventually. Probably not today, though. I'm tired and hungry, so I'm goin' home. Did you see Sheriff Glispin?"

Cap told him about the horse that had been stolen near Lake Crystal, and that Richard Roberts had shot two men out of the saddle, but the two got away.

George spit out another gob of juice. "Well, don't that beat all. You don't suppose them robbers come through here and stole my grays? Hell, them's work horses. Damn, I've got haying to do, don't they know that?"

Cap thought it strange that George should be more upset about getting his haying done, rather than the fact that perhaps two desperadoes had stolen his span of work horses.

"Too wet to hay anyway," said Cap, as if the sentence might ease George's concern.

"Yeah. Maybe you're right. Say hello to your folks next time you see 'em." George snapped the reins and moved on.

Cap went home, ate a hearty meal and slept good.

The next day was Sunday. Cap was up early, ate a big breakfast and packed some sandwiches, and this time took along some coffee and a coffee pot. If he was going to spend the entire day sitting in the rain, he figured he might as well have some comfort.

But the day did not present much comfort, since a thunderstorm loomed in over the area and seemed to hang for most of the day. Periodically the rain let up and gave him and the few other men with him the opportunity to see a few hundred yards down the road. A creek and a large meadow were across the road from them, but nobody had passed their way except Sheriff Glispin and two other riders who were patrolling the north-south picket line.

Cap had a single shot .44 caliber cap and ball rifle, which he doubted would fire because it was so wet. The two men with him had pistols. One had an old cap and ball revolver, the other had a rather new Colt .45, a fancy six shooter that fired cartridges.

During the entire day, the only thing that consistently came their way was the rain, and a lot of it.

For the next several days, the weather remained pretty much the same, though occasionally the sun came out, which was a welcome but rare sight. As miserable as the weather was, men volunteered in good numbers to help maintain the picket line. It was suspected the bank robbers might well pass this way, since on the way to the robbery, the same men, it appeared, had cased the area, checking out where bridges were located, where the best spots were to ford streams. Sheriff Glispin surmised that the robbers had located places where they might spend the night in relative seclusion. Relative seclusion meant the robbers more than likely paid good money ahead of time to people who would provide them with overnight lodging, no questions asked.

By Tuesday, no one was sure the robbers were anywhere near their locality. Word came that a few days earlier, two men had stopped at a farm a few miles northwest of Medalia to ask for directions. Later, the same day, the same two had asked for directions at a farm four miles west of Medalia. Both times they claimed they were after horse thieves.

By now there was no doubt in Cap's mind, and especially in George Rockford's, that the two gray horses he was missing had been stolen by the two robbers.

Still later, a report confirmed the two men had made it as far as Mountain Lakes, some 17 miles to the west, riding the two gray horses.

By Wednesday, reports came in that the desperadoes were on a path for Sioux Falls. That was eighty or ninety miles from their last reported location, and at least a two-day ride in this wet weather. The general consensus was that the robbers, as many as they were, had split up and eluded all the picket lines set up along the towns of Waterville, Madison, Mankato and Lake Crystal. As a result, Sheriff Glispin called off the search north of Medalia and everybody went home.

During the three weeks since the robbery occurred, any strangers who were found passing through the countryside came under severe scrutiny. All across Southwestern Minnesota, people were alerted to the robbery, and anybody who appeared remotely suspicious came under arrest. More often than not, various newspapers in the area were reporting "robbers caught at last." In due time, all suspicious characters were eventually cleared of any wrongdoing, except for two men, John Chafer and George Ranks, who, captured in St. Peter, actually turned out to be horse thieves.

Things had pretty much died down, and on Thursday afternoon, September 21st, Cap Pomeroy saddled up his horse and went to town. It wasn't a sunny day, but he consoled himself to the fact that at least it wasn't raining. He stopped at the J. N. Cheney Mercantile and asked an acquaintance of his, George Bradford, if he had heard any more news of the robbers.

George didn't know anything more than Cap, and was himself convinced the robbers, as incredible as it seemed, had managed to break through all picket lines.

"I think they lined up friends along the way to help them out if they got into trouble," George said. "I'm afraid they're long gone by now.

Cap agreed, and when George excused himself to wait on a customer, Cap hung around for a few minutes. He picked through some clothing, looked over the boot selection, not particularly interested in the items, but more in the possibility of catching a glimpse of the new young miss that had recently gone to work for the Cheney operation. But she did not appear to be working this day, so Cap went across the street to the barber shop for a haircut, his original plan.

Gerhard Brommel had a man in the chair when Cap walked in, so Cap took a seat by the window and gazed across the street at the Cheney Mercantile store, his thoughts focusing on the pretty face of the latest young lady clerk. He wondered what her name was. The family recently moved here from Minneapolis, and her father had something to do with the elevator, buying or selling seed, or both.

"I see you made the newspaper, Cap," said Gerhard as he brushed off his present victim with a hairbrush.

"Oh?" asked Cap, curiously.

"Ya. You, Pearson, Barnhardt, that young fellow Cassidy from St. Peter, and a lot more. You boys see anything on the picket?"

"Nope," said Cap. "Not a thing. Ducks is about all. Ducks in every pothole and marsh."

Gerhard motioned for Cap to get in the chair. "What's this I hear about Rockford's grays?"

"What?" asked Cap.

"Henry down at the telegraph, said a message came in the grays were found north of Pipestone."

"The hell you say?"

"Ya. Sent a description, and Rockford said they were his. He took off this morning in his buggy to go get them."

Cap was calculating how far it was from Medalia to Pipestone. "When did all this take place?"

"Last Sunday. Two fellows exchanged the pair of grays for a pair of blacks and rode off in the direction of Sioux Falls."

"Sunday?" Cap remembered the grays were stolen Saturday morning. The two thieves had covered a lot of territory in a short amount of time.

"Ya," went on Gerhard. "The telegraph said the grays were in tough shape."

"Have the two men been identified?"

"Nope. No one seems to know who they are. But these two fellows that was kilt in Northfield, they say they was from Missouri way. St. Louis police department confirmed that."

"Where did you hear all this?"

Gerhard pointed his scissors across the street. "The Colonel. Not much gets past his place. All the gossip collects over there."

Colonel Vought ran the Flanders Hotel. He was a former stage owner and driver, and in his later years he became the hotel host.

Gerhard produced a newspaper and gave it to Cap. He read the headlines. *Killer Robbers Evade Pickets. Disappointment is High.*

Cap began reading the article. Reports indicated the robbers had broken through all lines and were now presumed miles away from Medalia in Dakota Territory or Central Iowa. He continued reading, intent on reaching the point where his name appeared when suddenly Gerhard stopped cutting his hair. He and Cap peered through the shop window to the Flanders Hotel across the street. A young man, whom both recognized as Oscar Sorbel, had just ridden in, his horse lathered heavily and covered with mud. Colonel Vought met him outside and stood patiently as the young boy imparted some information, all the while gesturing wildly with his arms. He pointed back from where he came, and in seconds he jumped on his horse and raced down the street out of view.

"What do you suppose that was all about?" inquired Cap.

"Oh, another report, I suppose. The Colonel gets two or three a day from people who claim they seen the robbers. Everybody's thinking about the reward now. They say there's a thousand dollars on the head of each one of them."

"A thousand dollars?" remarked Cap. He knew there was reward money, but he had no idea the money was that high. That kind of money could be put to a powerful amount of use, especially when he compared it to the few dollars a month he was now earning on the farm place.

Gerhard clipped away, and Cap kept reading the paper.

Suddenly the door flew open and Sheriff Glispen burst in and glanced about the room. "Mr. Pomeroy, I can sure use your help. Young Oscar says they got em' spotted on the north fork by Doolittle's."

"Who?" asked Cap as he jumped out of the chair.

"The robbers. That your horse out front?"

"Yes!"

"Well, get it and come on. Gerhard, run down this side of the street and get anybody that wants to be a posse member."

"Yessir!" Gerhard answered as he ran out of the store.

"How many are there?" asked Cap as ran after the sheriff.

"Oscar said four of them, but could be more."

At the livery a few men had already gathered and were getting their horses ready. Others stood by uncaring, certain that the information delivered by Oscar Sorbel was nothing more than rumor, or at best, another erroneous account.

"Mount up!" the Sheriff hollered as he swung his horse around. "By Anderson's and Doolittle's! Let's go!"

Cap had left his horse across the street, and by the time he got hold of him and climbed into the saddle, the posse was already two hundred yards down the road.

He jammed his boots into the side of his horse, hoping to get a half way decent lope out of him, but his animal was basically a work horse, and running wasn't his style. He was also fat, since his best quality was grazing.

Cap had a head start on a few posse members, but in short time they all caught up with him, and he cursed his horse each time someone went by.

Within a few miles, the rest of the posse members were out of sight, and it was then Cap realized he didn't even have a weapon with him. Like all the others, he figured the robbers were long gone, and he had ridden into Medalia that day without a gun.

He remembered old Barney Camphor was a hunter, and when he reached the road to his place, he turned in and found Barney chopping wood. He quickly explained his dilemma, and Barney loaned him a double barrel muzzle-loading shotgun. Cap would have preferred a newer model with shells, but this was all Barney had. Barney also gave him his powder horn, his shot pouch and two caps, enough to give Cap another reloading.

With the shotgun firm in hand and the accessories draped over his head, Cap headed his horse back onto the road.

It was about three in the afternoon when he arrived at the north bank of the Watonwan River. On the other side he could see a high bluff, where a bend in the river formed a triangle of perhaps five or six acres. It was fairly level and open in some places, but one area was thickly covered with trees and brush. He could see riders congregating near that spot as he urged his horse into the water. Where he entered was quite deep, well over the belly of his horse. He raised his feet to keep them dry and at the same time worried the horse might fall into a hole and he would lose his shotgun. Just as bad would be if it got wet and couldn't be fired.

But he made it across safely and though he again kicked his horse, it was a futile effort. This animal was pretty well exhausted from the six-mile journey.

About 150 men had gathered in front of the thick facade of trees. Many others picketed the sides of the few acres, still others lined the far side of the Watonwan River. Captain Murphy, a former Civil War hero and a man whom Cap knew, was in charge. He, Sheriff Glispin and Colonel Vought were discussing the strategy they should take in routing the robbers. They were sure the robbers were at the end of this thicket, and now they knew there were four in number. Colonel Vought and several other members had chased them across the Watontan River into this area just minutes before Cap had arrived.

"I need volunteers!" Captain Murphy shouted above the crowd. "We're going in after them!"

Captain Murphy happened to be next to Cap when he asked for volunteers, and he noticed the double barrel Cap was carrying. "What's that loaded with?"

"Buckshot," said Cap.

"Mind if I borrow that?"

Cap was firm. "If this gun goes in, I'm going with it."

"Come on, boy, you're in."

Three other men volunteered. One was George Bradford from the Cheney Mercantile. George was a former school teacher, not the type of person Cap expected to join in a shoot out, but the man was determined, and he was carrying a long barreled rifle.

Benjamin Rice was a resident of St. Peter, a man Cap did not know, but he heard Captain Murphy tell Colonel Vought that although this young man was a mild mannered southern gentleman , he knew revolvers and weapons. He was a good shot and could be as reckless and damaging as the bullets of his Colt .45 pistol.

The seventh member was James Severson, a nineteen year old like Cap Pomeroy. He was wielding an older army musket, but he was anxious and willing.

Cap wasn't sure what he was getting himself into, especially after Captain Murphy started giving orders.

"These men are all armed and dangerous," said the Captain. "They already killed two men in Northfield, and they won't hesitate to shoot. You all understand me?"

There were no comments.

The Captain told the men to line up about ten feet apart, and Cap Pomeroy fell in to place at the center post of the line. "Take it slow," commanded the Captain as he drew his cap and ball pistol and pointed it into the brush.

The seven men started in, moving very slowly. Cap felt a heavy sweat roll over his face, and he suddenly wondered why he had volunteered. He certainly was no gunman, and he was carrying a weapon that he had never fired before. But there were more than a hundred men watching as he and the other six moved in, and he couldn't back out now for any reason.

The trees were thick, the ground marshy with a heavy growth of willows. Box Elders towered here and there, and wild plums and grapevines wrapped haphazardly in every direction making the progress extremely slow.

As he stepped forward, he could hear the crackling of brush as men along the line moved with him. He strained his eyes, looking for any movement through the thick foliage ahead, now placing each foot strategically. The air seemed suddenly hot and heavy as he made his way through the entanglement.

Captain Murphy was to his immediate right, he knew, but he could not remember who was off to his left. Though only ten feet away, he could barely make out the man. He was not sure how he would react when they routed the robbers, but he didn't have time to worry, since at that moment all hell broke loose!

On his far right, gunfire erupted. He heard several shots, one after another, and before he knew it, bullets whizzed above his head. He ducked down and buried his knees into the brush When the shots momentarily subsided, he barely had time to look up when another onslaught of gunfire broke out. Men off to his right of the line were giving return fire. The battle was in full force.

"Careful!" he heard Captain Murphy shout. Then he heard a shot twang as if it ricocheted off of a piece of metal, and he saw Murphy slump over.

"Are you okay!" Cap shouted.

"Yes!" came the reply.

For a few seconds the gunfire subsided, then abruptly more fire came from the direction of the robbers. Blue powder hung in the heavy haze, and Cap could now smell the acrid aroma. More shouts and commands echoed, but nothing was making any sense to Cap. His mind was on the fact that he had only two shots in his double barrel. How on earth would he find time to reload once he fired them both, and if he did fire them, would one of the robbers fire back? How many shots did they have to his two reports?

The gunfire was moving in his direction, and it appearedd the robbers had repositioned themselves, moving closer to the center of the line.

It was then he saw one of the robbers directly in front of him. He did not even aim, simply leveled the weapon at the man and pulled both triggers at the same time. He heard someone yell out, but he did not know if he hit the man or not.

More gunfire erupted, and he heard Captain Murphy give the command to close in. Cap had out his shot and powder and was reloading, surprised how calm he was. When the weapon was ready to fire, he pulled both hammers back, got to his feet and started forward again.

"Hold your fire!" he heard someone shout. "We give up!"

Cap moved in line with the rest of the posse and could now see where the bandits were positioned.

"Put your hands up!" Captain Murphy hollered at the men.

Cap saw one arm raised behind a clump of logs.

Immediately more fire broke out, all the shots coming from the line of the posse.

"We surrender!" he heard one of the men shout. "Goddammit, we surrender!"

"Put up all your hands!" shouted the Captain back.

"Can't!" came the retort. We're all down and I got only one good hand left!"

"Cap!" commanded Captain Murphy. "You put your shotgun on them boys, and if anyone of them moves, you give it to them, you understand!"

"Yessir!" answered Cap. He leveled the shotgun on the men huddled behind the woods and brush.

"Don't shoot," he heard one man say. This man had lost his hat and was baldheaded for the most part. Two other men were lying by his side, both wounded, both with bloody spots covering their slickers. The fourth man was flat on his back, dead from a blast of buckshot about the face and chest.

Cap Pomeroy had never seen a more bedraggled lot. These men were worn out, haggard, their faces tired and sagging, their eyes red from lack of sleep. They all had shaggy beards, and their clothing and boots were wet, soggy, worn, and caked with mud.

Their guns, eight total, mostly .44's, were collected and put in a pile. "What's your name," asked Captain Murphy of the older member, who obviously was the leader of the foursome.

"I'm Cole younger. These are my brothers Bobby and James."

"My God," said Captain Murphy. "The Younger gang!"

Cap's mouth hung open. He had heard of the Youngers, and here he was, in on the capture of them!

"Who's the dead man?" asked Captain Murphy.

Cole Younger stared at the man on the ground. "We don't talk about other members."

Cap looked down at the face of the dead man, tried to imagine what his features would be behind the heavy growth of beard.

Captain Murphy probed some more. "Mr. Younger," he addressed Cole, "We're on the trail of two others in the Sioux Falls area. Might they be Frank and Jesse James?"

Cap Pomeroy as well as other members of the posse were more than alert when they heard the names of the notorious outlaws and bank robbers.

"Well, now," Cole Younger answered, "we don't talk much about other members when they're dead, so we don't talk about them especially when they are alive. As far as I'm concerned, however, you caught all of us."

"There are at least two more, Mr. Younger," said Captain Murphy with a stern look.

Cole looked directly at Captain Murphy "I don't mean to be

disrespectful, sir, but like I said, as far as I'm concerned you caught all of us." He then looked at Cap Pomeroy. "Pretty young fellow to be chasing down men like us. Got to give you credit, all of you. You boys made a good day's wages. There's twenty thousand dollars on our heads dead or alive back in Missouri."

All of the men started talking among themselves when they heard that figure.

Other members of the posse now began appearing, and within a short time, they aided the Younger brothers to their feet and began escorting them back to the clearing. Cole had several minor wounds, none serious. Bob's arm had been shattered by a bullet in Northfield, and here in the final shoot-out he took a fresh wound in the chest.

James was hit the worst. He had five wounds, one very serious where a bullet had torn through his mouth.

While the others escorted the Younger brothers, Cap Pomeroy and another posse member picked up the dead man and carried him through the brush to a waiting wagon. On this man, Cap discovered a .32 caliber Smith & Wesson revolver. Someone knew this revolver had been taken from a member of the Northfield Bank.

Of the seven members who bravely walked into the woods, Bradford and Severson both were grazed by bullets. Captain Murphy had been hit, but the bullet struck his belt buckle, then ricocheted upward where it shattered his briar pipe. Later on he found the slug in his tobacco pouch.

The Younger brothers were held in the Flanders Hotel in Medalia until they were moved to Faribault for trial. The three received a life sentence and were sent to Stillwater State Prison.

And Cap, along with several other hundred men, waited patiently for word on who would share the reward for the capture of the Northfield bandits..

Author's note: The above story is a fictional account, to a certain degree, of Charles A. Pomeroy, known as *Cap* by his friends. He was a native of Medalia and one of the seven men who participated in the final shoot-out. The other six were the true names of his comrades. Little did these men know at the time that this incident would go down in history as *The Great Northfield Raid.*

The two men who escaped by stealing the set of gray horses from George Rockford were discovered later on to be, in fact, Frank and Jesse James, who eventually made their way back to Missouri via Sioux Falls, South Dakota.

After much litigation and a lapse of 1 1/2 years, Cap Pomeroy received $250.00 as his share of the reward money. The $20,000.00 reward for the Younger brothers offered by the state of Missouri was never paid, since their capture did not take place in that state.

Relatives of Cap Pomeroy strongly suspect Cap's buckshot was responsible for killing the one man in the final shoot-out, who was identified later as Charlie Pitts. Cap never acknowledged nor disclaimed that he fired the fatal shot, however, the only souvenir he kept from the robbers was Charlie Pitts' hat. After a few years he burned it.

Twenty years after the Northfield Bank robbery, Cap Pomeroy received a petition prepared for signatures of the seven members of the posse, asking for a full pardon of the Younger brothers, which he signed. Charles A. Pomeroy was 19 years of age when he participated in this escapade, and in 1942, when he died in Cleveland, North Dakota, he was the last living man of the seven posse members.

———— ♦ ————

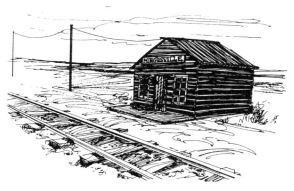

Saturday in Mingusville

The town, made up of a railroad station, a section house and a one and a half story saloon, lay along Beaver Creek among some rolling hills. The saloon was by far the most important building in this gnat of a community, in which the downstairs was for drinking and the upstairs for sleeping, if one had the courage to do so. The Mingusville Inn reminded one of a horse change station for a stage line, only because there was a good-sized corral behind it. However, the stage line never ran anywhere near this Montana edge of the Dakota Territory Badlands, and the only horses that inhabited the corral were Gus' matched pair of bays.

A lonely, dirt path led to the town, and anyone who lived within twenty-five miles knew, of course, where Mingusville was, but any passersby, who happened to be a few hundred yards off the dirt trail and didn't spot the railroad tracks, would easily have missed the entire three buildings.

Mingusville had a population of three—Henry Buckmiller who ran the railroad station and Minnie and Gus who ran the saloon, which sort of doubled for a post office. People who needed to send messages left them at the saloon, and eventually Minnie or Gus would run them over to the railroad station, and if Henry remembered to forward the message, it sometimes headed off in the next baggage car with instructions on where it was headed. Neither Minnie nor Gus ever recollected if anyone ever got a letter back, so it was difficult to ascertain whether the letter that was sent was ever received, but nobody seemed to mind.

None of the three inhabitants remembered Mingusville showing up on a United States map even though very few from the little community had ever seen a map of that part of the globe. It was possible the town may have appeared in an Atlas at one time or another during its short tenure, but more than likely by accident.

Gus proclaimed himself sheriff, mayor, postmaster and head barkeep of Mingusville, obviously named after him and his wife with his wife's name coming first in the name of chivalry. Minnie often doubled as the sheriff, postmaster and mayor whenever Gus was gone, which was only twice a year for supplies, but in the past whenever Gus was away, nothing out of the ordinary happened that forced Minnie to take on the extra duties.

If anyone showed up in huge numbers at the inn, it was usually on a Saturday, and today was Saturday. Huge in Bismarck might mean hundreds of people, but huge in Mingusville meant ten, maybe twelve individuals at the most.

On occasion, someone would happen by in a wagon and inquire about sleeping arrangements for the night, and if there weren't too many in the family, Gus and Minnie usually put them up for a small fee in the loft, which served as sleeping quarters and storage.

Gus was gone today, so Minnie was sheriff, postmaster, mayor and head barkeep. Saturdays were fairly routine. By mid afternoon, the cowboys from the C Bar C ranch usually arrived, six in all. They were a good lot, and Minnie liked them because they had a tendency to behave themselves. By ten in the evening, most of them would be heading back to their ranch, which was two hours north. By that time, two of the cowpunchers would still be fairly sober, two would be half in the bag and two would have already puked their guts out and would endure a miserable ride back home.

That's how the C Bar C boys were.

Melvin and Meldrum Barkley, two single brothers, usually showed up about five. They were the quietest of the lot, in fact, a bit timid. They owned a small acreage seven miles down along Beaver Creek, and on Saturdays they usually sat in a corner by themselves and drank beer all night long. Occasionally they indulged in cards, but neither of them liked to lose, so if they did play, they didn't gamble. It was hard to make conversation with them since they ran a pig farm, which wasn't very acceptable in this cattle-raising country. They both dressed alike with floppy black hats, checkered shirts and black pants, and both had full, curly beards. The first time Minnie and Gus set eyes on them, they mistook them for Mennonites that somehow had fallen away from the fold, but to their relief, they discovered later on they were just pig farmers.

About three o'clock, Saturday's activities were just beginning. Minnie heard shooting from down the road and knew the boys from the C Bar C were riding in. She stood in the doorway and waved as the six cowboys made their first pass, hooting and hollering, their six shooters blazing. At the railroad station, they all whirled around and raced their horses back to the inn. Since these were cattle ponies, the horses dropped their haunches when they stopped. On this occasion, little Billy Sparks slid up over his horse's head, made a summersault and splatted flat on his back to the ground. His horse backed up several yards, but little Billy hung on to the reins like a good cowboy should, until the horse dragged him to a stop.

The boys laughed and laughed, and though Billy was shaken and out of wind, his buddies pulled him to his feet and dragged him inside the saloon.

"Set 'em up, Minnie," said Tommy Gates, the leader of the pack. Minnie welcomed the boys, stepped up behind the bar and started pumping some cold beers. For the next half-hour, the beer kept flowing while the boys sat around and jawed, and later on they moved outside where they lined up bottles for a shooting contest. Laughter and gunfire filled the outdoors and hooting and howling filled the indoors when they all returned and forced the losers to buy.

At five o'clock on the nose, Melvin and Meldrum Barkley showed up and took their traditional places at a far table and watched the antics of the cowboys while they drank beer.

A short time later, the two Parker boys showed up, both wearing new black hats and red neckerchiefs.

"By god, if you ain't a pair of twins," one of the C Bar C boys quipped. Which one of you is Bubby?" Everybody laughed, since the two brothers were six years apart in age, one red haired, one a blond. If a cowboy couldn't tell which was which from five hundred yards, he either had to be drunk or dead or both.

One of the cowboys grabbed the new hats off their heads and tore out the door. "Come on, Tony," he hollered. "We got something new to shoot at!"

Four of the C Bar C boys held Bubby and Charles back while the other two fired their six shooters until they were empty. Of course, when they came back in, the black hats were still as new as could be with no holes in them.

Everybody howled including Bubby and Charles and Melvin and Meldrum, and Minnie pumped more beer.

Along about six, Alvin Huckstead arrived. When his big silhouette hit the doorway, he blocked out almost all the light coming through the frame. It would be difficult to find anybody within a hundred miles of Mingusville that was less liked than Alvin. He ran some cattle on his own ten miles southwest of town and occasionally showed up at the saloon. He was big, strong and obnoxious, especially after he had a few drinks in him. Alvin took a bath twice a year, and judging by the smell, the boys knew he was at least three months away from his next one. His beard was so scrubby and grizzled, the boys were sure he was growing something in it. The only thing the cowboys admired about him was the fancy pair of nickel-plated Colt six-shooters he wore in cross-belt fashion across his belly.

"What'll it be, Alvin?" asked Minnie.

"How 'bout startin' with a little kiss?"

He bellowed with laughter and a few of the cowboys laughed along with him, even though they did not consider the statement appropriate. Minnie was a fairly good looker for being in her mid forties even though she was a bit on the thin side. She overlooked Alvin's uncalled-for comment and raised a beer for him, and soon after, the boys in the bar were back to their crazy fun.

It wasn't long and Alvin was moving from cowboy to cowboy drinking his beer and bragging about a prize bull he bought in Medora from somebody passing through. "Man broke down with his wagon and needed money for repairs, so's I got his bull for practically nothin'. Yessir, sure took him!" Alvin prided himself on getting something for nothing.

On and on he went, bragging how his bull could impregnate fifty cows in an afternoon. "I named him Little Billy, after you," he said as he guffawed and slapped the little cowboy on the back. "Yessir, you boys should come over and watch him work. Maybe pick up some pointers." He would laugh some more, but he was the only one laughing at his crude jokes.

Coming from somebody else, the boys might have found the comments funny, but Alvin had a way of making everyone feel uncomfortable. He was unkempt, undereducated and undesirable. Privately, the cowboys referred to him as the big blow gut, but no one had the courage to tell him that to his face, mainly because they all knew Alvin could pound a wooden fence post into the ground with his fist.

"What d'ya say Little Billy?" Alvin went on. "'Bout time you bought the house a round of drinks, eh?"

Little Billy smiled and coughed when Alvin slapped him on the back again.

"Alvin, leave Billy alone," said Tommy Gates.

Alvin was feeling his beer now. "Well, what have we got here, Little Billy's protector?" He stuck his face right in to Tommy's, so close Tommy could smell his foul breath. "Whatcha gonna do if I don't leave him alone, hang me?"

Alvin whipped out both six shooters and fired them into the ceiling. He spun them once around his fingers and slipped them back into their holsters, and then laughed some more.

"Alvin, you behave yourself," said Minnie.

"Whoa, Minnie, gonna get the sheriff after me? Where is that badge totin' officer of the law?" he said as he looked about the room. "Hell, Gus's gone, so that makes you sheriff now, don't it Minnie? I ain't never been arrested by a woman law man."

He laughed some more and then went to pick on Melvin and Meldrum.

"He's getting a bit unruly, Minnie," said Tommy Gates.

"You boys just go on enjoying yourselves. Don't mind Alvin none."

"Melvin's gonna buy a round fer the house," hollered Alvin. "Aint'cha, Melvin."

"No, I'm not," said Melvin in his quiet voice. Alvin shoved Melvin backward and then started in on Meldrum. He threw an arm around him, gave him a big bear hug then suddenly stopped and was looking out the window.

"Well, what the hell we got here?" Alvin said loud enough for everyone in the bar to hear. The cowboys all moved to the window and saw the man arriving on a horse.

He wore khaki pants tied tightly about his legs and had a polished brown pair of stovetop, flat-heeled boots with funny-looking spurs. His fancy buckskin jacket had six-inch fringes running down each arm, along the bottom and across the chest and back. The stranger wore a pistol on his side, but a strap ran up over his shoulder and was attached to his pistol belt in military fashion, which the boys considered a rather unusual configuration. His hat was brown and straight brimmed with four creases in it.

"Ain't never seen a cowboy dressed like that," said Little Billy.

"Ain't never seen anybody dressed like that," said another.

When the man swung off the horse, he stood very straight, brushed his trousers a bit, then carefully tied his horse to the hitching post and tugged at the reins to make sure they were firm. He then pulled a carbine from the scabbard on his saddle and walked up the stairs to the door. As he stepped in, everyone inside simply gawked at him. He was a rather short man, a bit stocky and had a bushy brown mustache. His hands were covered with gauntlet gloves like the cavalry soldiers wore, but he definitely was not a member of the cavalry.

"Good day, gentlemen," he greeted as he touched the brim of his hat and gave a slight bow. "Good day, Madame," he said to Minnie when he saw her. "I trust you are the proprietor of this establishment?"

Minnie hesitated, curious at the high voice and the funny accent he had. "Yes, I am," she finally answered.

He spied a table off to his left and advanced toward it, then set his rifle against the wall and began removing his pistol and belt. "It is my understanding one can consume a meal here as well as imbibe in liquid refreshments."

Minnie was still gawking at him.

"Do you have a menu, Madame?" he said as he sat down

"No, but if you would like a bowl of stew, I can serve that up."

"That would be delightful," said the man with a broad smile as he expertly removed his gauntlets and placed them to the side. "Do you by perchance have a wine list, Madame?" he asked. And then he smiled again, realizing if he couldn't get a menu, a wine list was probably out of the question. "What select vintage wines do you have on hand, my dear?"

All the cowboys smiled and mumbled among themselves when they heard the words, *my dear.*

"Red or white," said Minnie.

"Red will be fine," said the man as he pulled a newspaper from inside his tunic and spread it out on the table. To the amazement of all, he procured a pair of round spectacles from inside his jacket and put them on. He proceeded to read for a bit and then looked up at all the men who were still staring at him.

"Something I can do for you gentlemen?" he asked.

The cowboys went back to the bar and Alvin sat down with Melvin and Meldrum again, his chair facing the stranger.

Minnie soon brought a glass of red wine and silverware and went back to the kitchen, and all the while, Alvin was watching every move the little man was making. First he smelled the wine, then held it up as if he were going to propose a toast, but instead he sipped a bit of it and appeared to rinse it around his mouth before he swallowed it.

He set the glass down and continued reading his paper. Moments later Minnie came in with a bowl of stew and some bread and butter.

"Anything else I can bring you, Mister?"

"No, my dear. Everything appears adequate and sufficient. Very good, indeed."

All the cowboys were now occasionally watching the stranger and curiously interested not only in his speech but also in his mannerisms as he dipped his spoon into the stew. None of the boys had ever seen a man spoon soup from the front of the bowl to the rear.

After a few spoonfuls, he would habitually touch the napkin to his lips, and not once did he slurp. He must have found the wine to his taste, since he asked Minnie for a second glass.

"Might I inquire of the contents of the wine, ma'am?" he asked as she poured it.

"Don't know for sure. Something Gus threw together a few months back."

The man smiled and nodded. "I am somewhat of an amateur connoisseur of wine, but please impart to Gus this wine has an excellent bouquet and a very succulent plum aftertaste."

"I will," said Minnie. When she returned to the bar she whispered to Tommy Gates, "Do you know what he said?"

"I think he likes it."

The cowboys started jabbering among themselves in voices low enough so the stranger could not hear.

"Who the hell is he?" asked one of them.

"Don't know," said another.

"I think I know," said Bubby Parker. He's that guy what

come from out east. He's got a place on the Little Missouri north of Medora."

"What's his name?" asked Tommy gates.

"I believe he's one of them Vanderbelts."

The boys once again focused their attention on the man in the corner when Alvin abruptly jumped up from his chair.

"Well, now," said Alvin in a loud voice as he paced about the floor. He directed his comments at the stranger. "What's all this about flowers and plum sucking?" He paced some more, then stopped and faced the man in the corner.

The stranger looked up and quite nonchalantly asked, "Are you addressing me, sir?"

"Well, I ain't talkin' to a little mouse in the corner." He turned to the crowd of onlookers. "Or am I?" He jerked with laughter as he took a couple big steps toward the man, and then mimicking the man's speech, he turned enough so the cowboys could see his antics. "Everything here still adequate and sufficient?"

"It has been up until now," said the man.

The cowboys all made faces and comments when they heard the man's retort.

"Whoa," said Alvin as he paced again. "Got a real gentleman here. Got a person here who sips his wine uppity-like."

"Alvin, you watch your manners!" scolded Minnie.

Alvin pointed his finger at her. "Minnie, you mind your own business!"

A few of the cowboys stood up and were about to say something. in her defense when Alvin shouted, "Sit back down!" He whipped out his two Colts, then turned to the man in the corner. "Now, mister, maybe you'd like to buy the house a drink?"

The man sat still, did not respond in anyway.

"I'm talking to you, four eyes," he said referring to the man's glasses.

The man looked sternly at Alvin, removed his glasses and stuck them inside his tunic, then slowly got up and walked up to the

158

big man.

"Well, now," said Alvin with a big grin. "Looks like our Mr. uppity is going to buy drinks for everybody."

The man looked up at Alvin, squared himself up and said, "Not exactly. You must understand, sir, I am not one to be intimidated."

The little man swung a fist so hard and fast into Alvin's face, he didn't even see it coming. Both of his pistols fired into the floor as he reeled back with the blow. The little man followed with a quick left and a final right-cross that snapped Alvin's head to the side with such a smack the boys were sure Henry could hear it from the railroad station. Down Alvin went and banged his head against the bar before he hit the floor, where he remained out cold.

Everybody in the bar whooped and hollered, and when the roar subsided, the stranger straightened his jacket, looked at Minnie and said, "My bill, please."

"You don't owe me a nickel, sir," said Minnie. "The performance you just gave us was certainly worth a bowl of stew and a glass of wine."

"Two glasses of wine, my dear," he said as he strapped on his pistol. He set his hat in place, picked up his carbine and headed for the door. "You'll have to excuse me," he addressed the crowd. "I must hasten forth, or I shall not reach my quarters before nightfall."

He turned to leave.

"You're welcome back anytime, Mr. Vanderbelt," Minnie hollered after him.

He turned to her. "Thank you for the invitation, my dear. And please be advised, the name's not Vanderbelt. It's Roosevelt."

Mr. Roosevelt tromped out the door, climbed on his horse and rode off.

The boys returned to the bar and looked at Alvin's limp body. "He sure packs a wallop for a little fella," said Tommy Gates.

"Maybe so," said another. "But I doubt he'll ever make it as a rancher."

"I'll bet he ran a dry goods store out east," said Bubby. "Anybody want to play cards?" asked Melvin.

Author's note: Theodore Roosevelt spent many years in the Badlands of North Dakota prior to his presidency. In 1884, he had an encounter with a drunk in Mingusville, which lies today in the heart of Wibaux, Montana, where he cold-cocked the ruffian. T.R was considered by the cowboys to be a rather strange adjunct to this frontier land, but after this incident got around, many took a different view. Teddy was an amateur boxer while attending Harvard, and during his presidency he lost the sight in one eye while sparring with a partner.

An Error in Judgement

They had seen the darkness move across the horizon at a rapid pace. For the past hour, the two rode at a quick trot, watching carefully, hoping the path of the storm would swing more to the east, but now they knew they were about to be caught up in it.

Yellow Eagle squinted, his eyes searching every direction. Out here on the plains, wind and snow that whipped across the barren landscape offered no mercy. A few trees were strung out along the narrow, frozen creeks, but nothing would lend the least bit of refuge.

Yellow Eagle turned to look behind him. "Grandfather, are you all right?"

The old man motioned with his hand to keep going, then once again bent his head down to protect himself from the pelting snow. He was dressed in a woolen jacket, canvas pants and leggings, and his hat was a floppy, worn piece of leather that did not cover his ears. Yellow Eagle had given him his blanket, but now even that was flapping uselessly in the wind.

Yellow Eagle moved on, fearing for his Grandfather now. He, too, was cold, not dressed as warmly as he should be in his buckskin clothing, but he at least had a fur-lined garment that fit over his head and offered some protection. His youth was in his favor against the bitter wind and snow, but his Grandfather was old and could no longer tolerate the cold like he once did in his younger years. When they had set out in the morning, the old man looked healthy and was riding upright, even singing in spite of the cold. But now, his frail body was hunched over his horse. Yellow Eagle thought by now he would already have found some shelter, but nothing presented itself. In the last few hours Yellow Eagle looked on pitifully as the cold slowly took its toll on the old man.

He wished he had held up and waited a day, but this storm had come up so suddenly, and it was becoming fiercer with every minute. It was a bad omen for him and especially for his Grandfather. The old medicine man could usually sense a storm three days in advance, but he too had been unable to predict the sudden arrival during today's journey.

It was another three or four hours to Slim Buttes where their Lakotah camp and safe refuge waited for them, but Yellow Eagle knew his Grandfather was not up to the ride.

In spite of the white wall of snow that confronted them, Yellow Eagle knew where they were, and as long as he kept to the trail along Antelope Creek, he would not get lost. Somewhere up ahead were small hills where the trees along the creek bottom might offer some shelter, but the storm was now raging, and he was not sure how far away the hills were.

He turned around and saw that his Grandfather's horse had stopped. Yellow Eagle went back and grabbed the reins of the horse and headed on into the bitter wind.

Evening was setting in, and the blowing snow now began to blur his vision. *Oh, Great Spirit, can you not provide us with refuge?* he humbly asked.

As they pressed on, ever so slowly the trail began to vanish, the way filled in with small snowdrifts. Yellow Eagle's hands were so cold he could hardly hold on to his rifle, and now as he tried to get a bearing on his location, he realized the river which he had been following was no longer off to his left. How long he had been riding and in which direction he was no longer certain, and the fear of being lost in this blizzard was quickly becoming a reality. This furious storm of white that the Great Spirit had suddenly cast upon them had become relentless and unforgiving. It now struck Yellow Eagle that *he* might survive this storm, but his Grandfather's safety was now a constant worry. He wished he had stopped earlier in the day at a place where there had been a few trees and brush, a place where they might have been able to ride out the storm.

Then, suddenly, no more than feet away, a large barn loomed before them. They had stumbled upon a white man's home on the prairie!

The wind and snow were fierce, and though he could not see the house that the white men lived in, he surmised it must be on the other side of this structure. Yellow Eagle did not hesitate. He dropped from his horse and opened the door to the barn, led the two horses inside and closed the door again. A dim light coming through a window allowed Yellow Eagle to barely make out the interior. Three horses were in stalls to his left and further on at the far end of the interior, a cow was tethered to a bunk.

He felt renewed energy as he helped his Grandfather down from his horse and laid him on some hay. The confines of this shelter were a gift from the Great Spirit, he was sure, and though they were free from the bitter wind and snow, the cold was now the enemy. Yellow Eagle removed his fur pelt and placed it over his Grandfather. The old man was shivering so fiercely, that before morning Yellow Eagle was afraid the Great Spirit would take him. And if that happened, what would the elders of his tribe think of him? Surely they would hold him responsible.

A terrible feeling of despair invaded his spirit as he pulled some hay around him and folded up into a fetal position to ward off the cold.

Inside the house next to the barn, Elsa Boulder removed three freshly baked loaves out of the oven and placed them on the table to cool, then glanced out the window into the frozen landscape. Darkness was moving in along with the howling wind. No less than three hours ago, Hank, her nearest neighbor, had stopped in to check on her, which he often did especially during the winter. He had left before the brunt of the storm hit, so he should have easily reached his farmstead by now, which was ten miles further west.

Elsa poked the stove and threw in a few more logs, and after she refilled the teapot with water, she sat down and gave a sigh of relief. She had been on her feet for the better part of six hours, and this respite filled her with a sense of accomplishment.

Elsa looked at the picture of her husband, Arden, who had died two years ago. During the first several months after his death, a simple glance at the picture used to bring on frightful tears, but now she had become accustomed to the loss. Arden had suffocated when the walls caved in on him as he dug a well. Hank always wondered why Elsa remained on the farm after the freak accident, but she loved this wide-open space in the Dakota Territory just as much as Arden did. The neighbors helped her with the spring plowing and planting and the fall harvesting, so her life continued on, except now she was without Arden.

She held the picture in her hands and let her mind wander back to that 4th of July celebration when Arden had swept her off her feet. The memory of that first meeting with him at the centennial event was as fresh now as it was five years ago.

The teapot whistled and brought her thoughts back to the present. She put the tea ball in the water and figured by the time she returned from tending her livestock, the tea should be through steeping. She lit a lamp, put on her coat and boots and gloves, then snugged Arden's leather hat in place and left the house. She entered the barn and set the lamp on a crate while she gave her cow some hay and oats. After that she grabbed a pitchfork and threw some hay to her three horses, and when she finished she suddenly noticed the additional two horses at the far end of the barn.

She was momentarily stunned, surprised she had not noticed them when she first entered. She held the lamp up and looked curiously about the barn in the dim light, but she could see nothing else. As she approached the horses, she could not help but wonder how they had entered the barn. They were laden with snow and frost about their manes and faces, and it was not until she was only a few feet away that she noticed a thin, braided leather bridle on each of their heads. As she came around the walled-off stall, the two Indians startled her.

She jumped back and froze in place, simply stared at the two. One was sitting upright, the other lay flat on the hay. She could see that the older man lying down was shivering heavily, and although a rifle was leaned against the wall, the other Indian made no attempt to reach for it.

The Indian sitting up motioned to his friend and placed his hands on the ground, at the same time speaking in his native language. She could not understand him, yet it was clear he was asking if they could stay the night. She had no objection, but the man on the ground was terribly ill and would need attention.

Elsa had no other choice. She motioned to them and spoke at the same time, "Come, come." Neither of them moved. "Come with me. Come," she said again as she beckoned for them to follow her.

They both finally understood, and after one man helped the other to his feet, the two followed her to the house. Elsa felt a slight sense of fear, but she could not in good conscience leave them out in this miserable cold.

Once inside she motioned to a cot on which the younger man helped the older lie down. When the man was comfortable, the younger Indian sat on a chair, and as he did so, his eyes focused behind Elsa to the pistol and holster hanging on the wall. She sensed what he was looking at, and again a mild fear struck her. It was Arden's pistol, and it was loaded, and she knew how to use it. As she removed her heavy clothing, she kept an eye on the man on the chair. He sat quietly, unmoving, his eyes a constant stare. Elsa had never seen an Indian from this close. He wore a band about his head, but unlike the old man, whose face was heavily wrinkled, his face was smooth.

She stoked the fireplace with more wood, and after warming up some soup she had made earlier in the day, she set a bowl of it on the table along with bread and utensils. The young Indian drank the tea down, then drank the soup straight from the bowl and tore off pieces of bread instead of cutting it. He ate half of the loaf and motioned for more tea and soup. The gesture seemed a bit abrupt, but Elsa assumed this might be customary among Indians to ask for more, so she gave him a second serving of each.

While the young man was eating, Elsa spooned soup into the old man's mouth and helped him drink the hot tea. Inside of an hour, both seemed considerably more comfortable, and understandably so since the warmth alone inside the house was as much of a healing factor as anything.

The old man soon fell asleep, but awoke a short time afterward and beckoned for more soup. As she continued to feed the ailing man, she began to scrutinize her unexpected guests. In the back of her mind she felt a sense of distrust having these two strangers in her home, yet, the young man at the table had not made any threatening gestures of any sort. It was strange how rigid he sat, how tense, as if at any moment he would spring out of the chair.

He was quite a bit younger than the man on the cot, and his buckskin clothing and leggings fit him well. However good they may have been for repelling snow, she did not think they offered much warmth. But, maybe she was wrong.

The old Indian on the cot had hair streaked with gray that went along with the age old lines in his face, but his clothes were much like what Arden used to wear. His shirt was colorful, the pants were made of canvas cloth, and his coat appeared to be wool. The only clothing on him that seemed Indian-like were his leggings. She also noticed that neither of the men had gloves.

She wished she could converse with them, but as the night wore on, silence continued to be the norm, except for the ever-present howling wind. After some time, and to break the monotony, she finally said to the young man as she pointed to herself, "I am Elsa. My name is Elsa."

He repeated the name a few times until he knew it, and although he pronounced his name in his native tongue, she had no idea what it meant. He sensed that, and seeing a pencil and paper on the table, he drew a crude picture of an eagle. He held the picture up against the yellow curtain at the window and nodded as he motioned back and forth from the curtain to the eagle.

"Yellow Eagle," she said gleefully. "You are Yellow Eagle?"

He made a face as if he did not know what she meant, but then he grunted and repeated in broken sounds, "Yel-low-Ea-gle."

Yellow Eagle it was, she determined, but that was the extent of their conversation.

She dozed for a few minutes while sitting in her chair and woke to see Yellow Eagle putting more wood on the fire. He was not a big man, but he was muscular, and as he bent over the hearth she thought about her husband for a moment, remembering how he too, in the middle of many wintry nights, had often got up to feed the fire.

He returned to his chair and motioned that she could go to sleep and that he would tend the fireplace, but Elsa was not sure she should to do that. Still, they did not at all seem like savages as some of her neighbors claimed the Indians were.

The last time she had even been near Indians was well over a year ago at the trading post on the Moreau some twenty miles to the southwest. On occasion she had spotted small hunting parties on the south side of Antelope Creek, but they had always kept their distance from the homestead. She guessed these two men were probably Lakotah Sioux, members of a band that lived in the Slim Buttes area to the west. Hank's farm was as close to Slim Buttes as any farm was, and he had never had any trouble with the Indians, so why should she?

She became so tired, and now feeling a bit more at ease with the two men, she retreated to her bedroom and closed the door. However, once inside she propped a chair against the door and kept Arden's Winchester next to her bed.

Sleep finally came, and when she woke she discovered the two Indians were gone. She looked out the window toward the barn, which she could see now, and though the wind had dissipated, the snow was still coming down. She was certain Indians knew more about weather than she did, and she guessed they probably left because they sensed the main storm was over. She wondered how long they had been gone, and though she could see as far as the creek a quarter of a mile away, they were nowhere in sight.

When she looked about the room, nothing seemed disturbed, and Arden's pistol and holster were still hanging on the wall. Suddenly she saddened, realizing she had made an error in judgement concerning the two. There had been no need to be fearful of the Indians. They had accepted her hospitality like she would have offered anyone, and then they simply moved on. She was glad she had helped them, and that thought alone provided her with a good feeling of contentment.

She dressed and ate a quick breakfast, then donned her winter clothes and headed for the barn. Her jovial mood continued as she slid the door open and went inside. Her cow was in the stall and turned her head expecting some oats, but Elsa stopped in her tracks and gasped as she stared at the empty stalls.

Her three horses were gone! She opened the far door and ran out thinking the three may have got out when the Indians left, but they were gone. Though snow was still falling, she could still see depressions where the five horses had left the barn, their tracks all leading south toward Antelope Creek.

She had made a terrible error in judgement. "My God!" she screamed out into the cold. "You stole my horses! I gave you shelter and food and you stole my horses! Damn you! Damn you!"

She collected her thoughts. Two days ago her cattle had been grazing on the north branch, and with them were her two workhorses. She grabbed a halter from the barn and set out across the frozen land, and inside of an hour she spotted her cattle and the matched pair of Percherons in a draw near a frozen creek. She walked right up to Paddy and put a halter on him, then lined him up next to a downed tree, stepped up on the log and jumped on his back. Once in place, she nudged him on toward the farm as Curly, the other Percheron, fell in behind.

At the barn, she put a bridle and saddle on Paddy and left Curly in one of the stalls. She led Paddy to the house where she strapped Arden's holster and pistol on under her coat and slipped his Winchester into the scabbard on the saddle.

She hoisted herself up onto the back of the sixteen hundred pound horse and headed off towards Antelope Creek. Paddy moved easily through the snow. He had hooves so large, it was as if he were walking on snowshoes. Walking was his normal gait, but with a little prodding he finally skipped into a trot, a gait he could maintain all day without tiring. He was a much rougher ride than any of the saddle horses, but he was gentle and reliable, and for that she was most thankful.

She cursed herself and the Indians as she rode along the creek following the faint tracks. The Indians were moving along single file, so it was difficult to count the horses. After some time she wondered if it were possible the horses simply wandered off and followed the two Indians. She discounted that thought since loose horses rarely walked one behind another, and anyway, whenever her horses had got out before, they simply hung around the home place.

These tracks were headed in a westerly direction, which would eventually lead to the Slim Buttes area. She cursed the two Indians some more, angered that they would turn on her like that. Arden had once told her that although Indians might give the appearance of friendship, one still had to be on guard. Indians liked horses, especially fine, well-bred horses, and stealing one was an act of courage and bravery. She should have paid more attention to that simple advice, since these three horses were Arden's pride and joy. She had to get the horses back, if not for herself, at least for Arden.

Elsa was furious with herself for being so naïve, yet somehow she could never have left the Indians in the barn where the sick man was sure to freeze to death. Arden wouldn't have. Still, how cowardly they were, what audacity they possessed.

"Damn you two!" she hollered out again.

In short time, the trail of tracks became more visible. The Indians had crossed a narrow part of the creek and broke through in a few places where the ice was thin. She prodded Paddy across and could see where the horses had emerged on the other side. Here, the snow was more compact, and now she could see their tracks far ahead along the south side of the creek. She pressed Paddy on and constantly searched the horizon, hoping she might catch a glimpse of them.

She rode on, and in a draw with some trees she found where they had stopped momentarily. Here, the hoof prints in the snow were very clear. For a few hundred yards, the horses had trailed one behind another, but then they had spread out some, and she could discern the tracks of five different sets of prints.

There was no doubt now, as if there ever had been. She looked about getting her bearings and realized the Indians were headed in the direction of Hank and Verna's place. She urged her horse on anxious to reach their farm and even managed to get Paddy into a lope. She was sure Hank would join her and help try to catch the thieves before they reached the buttes.

As she rode, she wondered what she would do if she accidentally caught up to them. She had the Winchester with her and was mad enough to use it if they resisted. But if by chance she did manage to catch up to them, she wondered whether they would shoot at her, or would they leave the horses behind and hightail it for the safety of their camp?

She kept asking herself what Arden would do under the circumstance, but the more she thought about it the more confused she became.

She realized now the snow had stopped falling and she could see a good distance ahead. They were definitely following Antelope Creek, which led to south end of the Slim Buttes hills. The buttes extended to the north for ten or fifteen miles, and anywhere inside them the Indians would find their safety. If they made it that far she did not think Hank would chance to follow them, since the buttes were the Indians' domain in this region, and hundreds of the Lakotahs would be camped there. It would be foolish to even think of trailing them in.

Inside of another fifteen minutes, she came within sight of Hank's farmstead. The tracks of the horses led upwards to her left on a rise away from Hank's place, but she stayed along the bottomland. Once she joined up with Hank, they could easily find the trail again.

As she came over the last rise and headed down toward the farm, she could hardly believe her eyes. Her three horses were tied up outside Hank's barn alongside a pair of saddle horses! When she rode into the yard she was not surprised to see Bill Ringer walk out of the barn with Hank. Bill's acreage was a few miles north of Hank, and quite often the two ran their cattle together.

"Elsa," Hank greeted. "Me and Bill was just about to head over and bring your horses back."

Elsa stepped off Paddy and looked over her three prize beauties. "Where did you find them?"

"This mornin' me and Bill was on the south range checkin' out our cattle and we seen your horses strung out behind two fellers. We figured they was stealing 'em, so we rode after 'em."

"And?"

Bill Ringer went on. "We hollered for them to stop, and if they would have, they might have fared better."

She looked at Hank. "They fired first, Elsa. We shot em' both right off their horses."

"Are they dead?"

"I'm afraid so. Got 'em laid out in the barn. Don't quite know what to do with 'em. Ain't no law around here to report 'em to."

Elsa went numb. She had cursed the Indians all the way here, and though she had judged the two Indians wrongly, she was still sorry they were dead. Neither Hank nor Bill Ringer had any idea she had given them refuge at her farm home, so how could she expect them to understand her sorrow?

"Can I see them?" she asked.

Hank made a face. "Elsa, it ain't a pretty sight."

"I... want to see them."

Hank nodded, led the way to the barn where the two men were laid out flat on their backs.

She stared at the two bodies and burst into tears.

"Elsa, I'm so sorry," said Hank as he grabbed her and held her in his arms. "I should'a never let you see 'em."

"No, no!" she said as she pulled away from Hank and once again stared at the two men. "They're not Indians!"

"No," said Hank. "Just a couple of horse thievin' drifters. What's this about Indians?"

She didn't know whether to laugh or cry as she stared at the two dead white men.

Hank and Bill had the most puzzled looks on their faces. "Why don't you come in the house for a spell. You'll feel better."

She went inside and stayed for lunch, and stayed long enough to tell them about Yellow Eagle and his friend, to whom she had given protection during the storm.

In the middle of the afternoon, she headed back with her three horses trailing behind. When she reached the farmstead, she went directly to the barn, threw open the doors and led her three horses inside. She was startled for a moment as she looked up at a buck deer hanging from a rafter. It had been gutted, and stuffed into one of the ears was a rolled up sheet of paper. She unfolded it, and there was the drawing of the eagle the buckskin clad Indian had made the day before.

"Please forgive me, Yellow Eagle," she said as she broke into tears. She cried and cried, she was so happy.

Captain Durant's Last Stand

The new fort was built near the confluence of the Missouri and the Yellowstone Rivers, a strategic location in the extreme northwest corner of the Dakotas. The row of officers quarters presented a majestic appearance, their whitewashed exteriors a stark contrast to the brown, brome grass on the vast plain beyond.

This was a typical fort with a barracks, a blockhouse, an icehouse, farrier and livery buildings and various other structures that housed ammunition and additional cavalry equipment on this lonely outpost.

Inside the headquarters building, the commander of the fort had assembled his officers for another one of his impromptu sessions. He was a tall, well built man for being near sixty, with white hair and a Norwegian face made of iron.

"I want to thank you gentlemen for the diligent devotion you offered during the reconstruction of this facility. General Grant himself would be proud of your efforts. I've asked him to pay a visit, which he said he would do just as soon as he can tear himself away from the office of the presidency."

A few of the officers chuckled at his humor, a word that just barely existed in his vocabulary. Brevet General Bjornson arrived almost a year ago and had gained an immediate reputation for initiating work details that were virtually non-productive.

He had bucked army rules and ordered the officers quarters to be painted an off-gray color with a crimson trim. When it was pointed out that army regulations forbid anything else but white, he flew into a tantrum and berated the officers who had discovered the inconsistency. Eventually he relented and the quarters were repainted, but only after the post chaplain had a word with him.

On another occasion he had sent a detail of four enlisted men out early one morning with a wagon and told them, "Be back at noon with a full load of wood or don't return at all!"

Fearing repercussions, they decided not to return, so a detail of fourteen men was assembled and sent out to find them. Of the fourteen, four more men disserted once they were far enough away from the fort.

The insane recommendations seemed to be unending. During a near blizzard in March, the entire post was ordered to hold a dress parade. The officers and men were to *pretend* prominent visitors were present for review. After standing at attention for almost an hour on one of the coldest days of the year—and without gloves, since the general thought his troops were tough enough to endure such conditions—fifteen men were treated for minor frostbite.

On another insane spring day, he ordered a scouting detail to cross the Missouri to the north, to determine whether there was a buildup of hostile Indians. But the Missouri at that time of year was ravaging, high water. It was impossible to cross the river even with a raft, so how could the Indians possibly get across to attack, he was asked.

That had almost cost Captain Durant a reduction in rank. Other officers came to his defense, which saved him from the humility. Such were the directives coming from the commander in charge. The officers as well as the enlisted men found his inane recommendations a source of conversation, which if nothing else provided the usually boring nights with some comic relief. Privately, the General had become the brunt of many jokes. There was a time, the officers admitted, when the man had probably been a good commander, during the Civil War, for example. But they also believed that since then he had lost touch with reality. The base brig always seemed to have someone in its confines, someone who had shirked his duty in one way or another. But in the eyes of Captain Durant, no one on this post, which was so remote from civilization, needed to have his duty lowered any more than it already was by doing thirty days in jail.

So now, Captain Durant sat with his peers, all wondering what new challenge the General would present today.

The answer came immediately.

"Gentlemen, in return for your hard work at making Fort Buford the bastion of defense that it is, I am recommending a buffalo hunt."

The officers exchanged glances and muttered among themselves at the thought.

"I've been informed by Jassom, our post interpreter, that a large herd of buffalo has been sighted no more than fifteen miles to the west along the Yellowstone. I want a detail sent out to return with enough buffalo tongue and hump to feed the entire post."

"Just the tongue and hump, sir?" asked Lieutenant Ihry.

"Yes. We all know the Indians consider those to be the choice parts of that hairy beast. They would be a delicacy for the men and at the same time raise moral."

"What about the rest of the meat?" asked the Lieutenant.

"What about it?" he snapped back.

Captain Durant came to the Lieutenant's aid. "General, it will require fifty or sixty buffalo to feed our men just tongue and hump. Could we not serve steak as well? That way, we could get by with maybe a half dozen buffalo."

"Leave the rest on the prairie to rot."

"But sir, the Lakotah are depending on the herd for their fall hunt. If we..."

"Captain Durant, do I understand you are defending these red savages?"

"Sir, I think they..."

"Captain Durant, you will head up the detail and take Lieutenant Ihry with you. Have Sergeant Halloway get a troop together and draw enough provisions for two days. Any questions?"

He didn't wait for an answer. "Good. Dismissed."

All the officers slowly shuffled out of the headquarters building, shaking their heads, their comments low enough not to be overheard. Captain Durant and Lieutenant Ihry headed across for the barracks. "What insanity," he said to the Lieutenant. "Dig up Sergeant Halloway, find Jassom and see if he will come along. We're going to need an interpreter."

"You think we'll run into Indians?"

"Where ever we find buffalo, you can bet we'll find Indians. I'll meet you at the livery."

Just short of noon, the small column left the fort. The two officers took the lead, followed by Jassom, the civilian interpreter who drove the supply wagon. Jassom was a small, stocky man with a thick beard and a personality like a bull buffalo. At his side was his .54 caliber long barreled buffalo gun.

Behind him was Sergeant Halloway and thirteen mounted soldiers that the Sergeant had handpicked, all good shooters in his estimation.

By late afternoon, the troop had covered fifteen miles and sent scouts out ahead, but no buffalo were in sight. The men set up a perimeter line, assigned night guards and spent a peaceful, but very cool night on this late, September outing.

At sunrise after a meager breakfast of biscuits and bacon, the column was on the road again, and by noon had struck the Yellowstone. Again, scouts out front had not yet spotted any buffalo. The column stopped and sent more scouts to the south, but without any luck.

On the third morning, Captain Durant became concerned. They had provisions for only two days, and by now the General was probably pacing in his quarters, wondering where the troops were.

In the late afternoon, now nearly forty miles from the fort, they came upon some Indians. Jassom was the first to spot them—three warriors astride their ponies on a hillside well over a mile away, all apparently staring back at the column.

"Get a horse, Jassom, and come along with me," the Captain commanded.

Jassom borrowed a trooper's horse, and in no time the two were headed up the long, sloping hill toward the ridge.

"I think that's Old Red Feathers," said Jassom.

"Suppose he'll parley with us?" asked the Captain.

"Long's I'm with you, you ain't got no fear." Then he added. "Course, he don't particularly care for men dressed in blue, but then he's usually reasonable fer the first couple minutes."

Captain Durant felt a slight lump in his throat. He had never been this close to an Indian before.

The two slowed when they reached the three Indians. Two were armed with bows, and Old Red Feathers was carrying nothing more than a lance. They were dressed brightly in buckskin clothes, warm wear for this time of year. At least they weren't wearing war paint, the Captain was thinking, however it did appear Old Red Feathers had a couple scalps attached to his lance.

Jassom made a peace sign, and Old Red Feathers returned the same sign, which gave the Captain a sense of security.

After a short conversation between Jassom and Old Red Feathers, Jassom turned to the Captain. "He wants to know what brings you onto his land?"

"Tell him we want to hunt buffalo."

Jassom interpreted for Durant, which drew laughs from all three.

"Tell him we need to shoot about fifty buffalo. We'll take only the tongues and humps and he and his people can have the rest. Tell him when we find the herd, we'll set up a stand and bring down as many as we can without stampeding them. See if he'll go for that."

Jassom again interpreted. "Red Feathers says you want the choicest parts. He asks why that is."

Captain Durant thought a moment. "Tell him that at least

once a year, even a white man likes to eat as well as the Indian."

Jassom gave the information word for word. Old Red Feathers simply grunted. "He doesn't believe you."

"Then tell him it wasn't my idea. Tell him the command came from our leader who is known among our people as the Great White Crazy Chief."

The three Indians laughed and nodded when Jassom interpreted. "They believed that," said Jassom.

"Tell him after we have our meat, I'll give him a rifle and 50 rounds of ammunition."

Jassom made a face. "What's the General gonna say 'bout that?"

"He ain't gonna know. Tell him."

Jassom told him. "It's a deal." Jassom exchanged a few more words with Red Feathers, and then said, "The herd's 'bout an hour and a half ride to the south. His people will be on the move come daybreak."

"Tell him we'll be there."

Early the next morning, the troops were on the move headed in the direction Red Feathers had indicated the day before. Jassom met with Red Feathers when the buffalo herd came into sight, and between the two of them, they selected an area where some of the troopers could reach unseen to within one hundred yards of the center of the herd.

The spot Red Feathers selected was behind a rise, downwind from the herd, which was absolutely necessary, since the report of the rifles would, with a little luck, be muffled enough not to startle the herd. Jassom knew his stuff. In his younger years he had done many such buffalo stands shooting on his own. His record, he claimed, was twenty-six buffalo at one setting before the herd stampeded.

Jassom and five troopers, all armed with .54 caliber rifles, stealthily made their way up a rise until the buffalo came into view. With a stiff wind blowing in their faces, Jassom gave the command for the troopers to shoot one at a time.

In succession, they began firing, one after another, only a few seconds in between rounds. The buffalo slumped on the prairie one after another. The delight of the kill swept over Red Feathers' face like a fresh snow covers the land. This was new to him, since his tribal members had very few rifles, mostly small caliber, and relied mainly on the use of bows and arrows for the hunt.

The men kept firing again and again until finally the herd stampeded.

"Shoot at will!" Jassom hollered. The cavalry sharp shooters kept up as fast as they could reload. Now, on the far side of the herd the warriors from Red Feathers' tribe were on horseback, giving chase effortlessly, releasing their arrows as fast as they could.

The thundering herd headed off to the south, their resounding hoof beats slowly fading amid yelps from the ensuing Indians.

Jassom and his men stood up and counted fifty-seven buffalo on the ground before them. In less than five minutes of shooting, six men had brought down more buffalo than Red Feathers and his members could ever hope to kill during an all day pursuit.

"Get the rest of the men up here and let's skin 'em up," commanded the Captain.

Red Feathers had never worked side by side with the blue coats, and the last thing he expected was to be involved in a buffalo hunt with them.

He beckoned his tribal members to come forward. The Lakotah women slowly approached from across the way and finally advanced the last several yards when Red Feathers shouted at them, telling them it was all right to begin skinning the animals. Red Feathers was delighted with the results, chatting with his people, giving instructions and commands. When Jassom had the wagon brought up, everyone—cavalry men beside Indians—was busy cutting out the tongues, skinning the hides and removing the choice humps of the animals and placing them in the wagon box.

At that moment and unknown to Captain Durant and his men, Brevet General Bjornson and an aide sat on a hill several hundred yards away, peering through field glasses at the event below. Four days had passed since Captain Durant and the column had left the fort, and now, the General and a twenty-man troop had followed up, suspecting Durant and his men had run into trouble.

"What the hell are they doing?" the General asked the young officer.

"They're skinning the buffalo, sir."

"Alongside the enemy? I can't believe it, my own men helping the enemy." He dropped his glasses. "Get my horse up here, and be quick!"

In moments, his aide brought up two horses. The rest of the column remained out of sight as the two started down the hill toward the wagon.

As the General and his aide approached, Red Feathers and his tribal members raised up, curious to view this man that the blue coats labeled as the *Great White Crazy Chief.*

"Captain Durant!" the General fumed. "What in the hell do you think you're doing?"

"Sir, we're acquiring buffalo tongues and humps like you ordered."

"You are aiding the enemy, Captain!"

The General's eyes were piercing, his iron face a wrinkled rage. "Captain Durant, you are under arrest." No one moved, no one responded.

He turned to his aide. "Lieutenant, arrest this man!"

"Sir?" the young Lieutenant said. He shrank back, unsure what he should do.

"Arrest him! Arrest Captain Durant!" He glared at the Captain. "You're aiding the enemy!"

"*You* are the enemy," said the Captain as he drew his pistol. The Colt barked loudly on the open plain and echoed along the hillside. The bullet struck the General in the chest and knocked him from his horse. He was dead when he hit the ground.

The men were stunned. No one moved, no one even went to

the General's side to aid him in case he wasn't dead. Captain Durant calmly put his pistol back in the holster, then climbed onto his horse and looked over the crowd. Red Feathers and his people were as still as posts.

The Captain looked directly at Jassom. "See that Red Feathers gets his rifle and cartridges." He looked at the rest of his men. "*I* killed General Bjornson. Don't make up any stories that the Indians killed him. *I* killed the General. You can report that to the authorities."

He spurred his horse into a lope and rode through the downed buffalo, past Red Feathers, past the many women who stood near him. Everyone watched as the Captain crossed the narrow valley, watched until he and his horse went over a hill out of sight.

A report was made when the soldiers returned to the fort and a warrant was issued for Captain Durant's arrest. A detail was dispatched to track down the Captain, but none of the men made much of an effort to seek him out or even learn of his whereabouts. Inside of two weeks, the detail came back with nothing to report.

During the ensuing years, no one ever saw Captain Durant again, or even heard anything about him.

And no one missed General Bjornson.

Two Bears and Tate

Two Bears had been watching the campsite across the river, his keen eyes taking in every move the trapper made. He was gaining knowledge about the trapper's routine and carefully observing the white man's habits. Over the past three days Two Bears had learned that the man rose shortly before sunrise every morning. Right afterward the man would stoke up his campfire and cook an early morning meal, which consisted of some meat and an assortment of other foods with which Two Bears was not familiar.

Two Bears did not know who the man was or where he had come from, but he guessed the man had been here for some time, and he knew the man spent his days trapping along the horseshoe bend of the river. Each day he made inspection of his traps, and during the last three days, Two Bears had seen the man skin out nine beavers and three mink. Where the man kept his pelts cached, Two Bears did not know exactly, since each day the man disappeared into the trees and thick brush with the pelts in various directions from his camp. The man had set up his camp in a very secure and confining spot, exactly what Bears would have done if he were a trapper.

A heavy growth of underbrush and trees concealed Two Bears' location from where he could secretly observe the white man's camp. The river between him and the trapper was not very wide, less than a two minute swim across, and the current, though fairly swift, was not a deterrent for the Blackfoot Indian. Two Bears was a good swimmer in spite of his slim build, and a strong man who had won many contests in his village whenever strength and endurance played an important role. He was an excellent horseman and a very good marksman with his bow and arrow.

The distance across the river would test the marksmanship of a well-placed arrow, but Two Bears was confident that he could hit the man across from him if the wind wasn't such a deterrent. A high bluff off to his left seemed to form a constant downdraft, which intermittently diminished in strength without warning. At such moments when an arrow was in flight, an abrupt change in the wind alone could easily throw the arrow off course and cause it to miss its mark.

Killing the man by arrow was probably not the best course, but killing him could be a simple matter, thought Two Bears. In the night he could slice the trapper's throat with his knife or bludgeon him with his war mallet. However, a much more honorable feat would be to simply steal the man's horses without killing him, something he could boast about for years to come, and his people would believe him, because he was an honorable warrior with much credit to his name.

And so Two Bears decided he would not kill the man.

He was not remotely interested in the white man's beaver or mink pelts, but he could easily visualize himself as the owner of the man's three horses—animals worthy of much praise. The three animals were held in a rope corral beyond the white man's tent, barely visible even now. They were magnificent beasts, such as he had never seen before, so much taller than his own prized paint, which was now tethered a five-minute walk away behind him. Two of the horses had four white feet and long white blazes on their foreheads, which made Two Bears believe that they were perhaps twins, or at least born of the same mare. The third was solid black with several white spots on his rump. This black horse was not unlike the excellent riding horses the Nez Perce tribes to the south and west of his village bred.

All three of these horses would bring Two Bears much honor

if he were able to return to his village with them. Just one of the three would be a definite prize, certainly equal to his own horse.

But there were some obstacles to all the observations Two Bears had been making. Whenever the man left his camp, sometimes he returned almost immediately, sometimes he would be gone for a longer period of time.

Sometimes he took his three horses with him when he left the camp, sometimes he took only one, and occasionally he left all three horses when he checked his traps.

Every night, the man seemed to bed down in a different spot, which might be an arrow's distance from his campfire or only a few feet away. Two evenings ago Two Bears observed where the trapper had laid out his bedroll, but by the next morning, he emerged from a different direction, which meant he had changed his location during the night.

At the next sunrise, the three horses were nowhere to be seen, but by mid morning, the trapper appeared bringing the three horses with him, which meant during the night he had moved their location.

The man was smart and cunning by changing his routine, which irritated Two Bears terribly and gave him a great deal of frustration. At the same time, Two Bears admired the white man's ingenuity. This white trapper was alone on the edge of Blackfeet territory, a brave thing for a handful of trappers, but an extraordinarily brave deed for a lone trapper.

Two Bears continued to stare through a narrow slit of tree branches, sure his position was secure, sure the man across from him did not have the remotest idea he had been observing him. The trapper, now stoking his fire, was clad in buckskin clothing and had leggings, which ran up to his thigh, and he was wearing moccasins. He wore a floppy hat with a brim, it too made out of leather, Two Bears thought. The man had a full beard, and though a bit heavy set, he seemed to move with ease about the camp. The trapper also had a rifle and carried a pistol and knife on his belt at all times. Two Bears did not know much about the white man's weapons, other than the rifle could be a single shot or it could be one, which had many bullets. He had no idea what sort of pistol the man carried, but he suspected it too might have many bullets. How such weaponry functioned he did not understand, but he feared the weapons more than anything. He knew that after the man fired either weapon, a stream of smoke spewed out followed by a small clap of thunder, which could carry a bullet into the heart of a man a long distance away, much beyond the reach on one of his arrows.

Two Bears kept his gaze on the man, watching every movement. He wondered where the man would sleep tonight, and he hoped it would be far enough away from camp on this evening. The moon was in a half-full phase, but for the past two nights the sky had been overcast, allowing him absolutely no night vision. If by chance the clouds dispersed this evening or even thinned, under the light of a half moon, he would make his move, and by morning the horses would finally be his.

It had occurred to Two Bears that he could return to his village and get other braves to help him acquire the horses, but that would mean a nine day round trip, and the trapper might be gone by then. It also meant he would have to share the horses with his fellow tribal members, so he made up his mind that he alone would steal them.

Two Bears kept watching. The man was still stoking his fire.

———— ♦ ————

Across the river, the trapper, who simply went by the name of Tate, threw a few more pieces of wood on the fire. As soon as the wood turned to cinders he would cook the fat beaver tail as his evening meal, and then he would settle down for the night.

For the past three days he had been carefully and curiously observing the lone Indian. Even now, as he chanced a glance across the river, he knew the Indian was hiding behind a pile of brush and was sure the man was watching his every move. He was surprised the red man had not tried to steal his horses already, for he knew the Blackfeet Indians prized good quality horses. Any Indian did, for that matter, and of course, if a warrior could steal horses and return to his village with them, he would receive much honor.

Tate had considered the possibility that the Indian might try to kill him with a well-placed arrow from across the river, but Tate also knew that the high bluff off to his right created a swift wind, which flowed down over the river surface at a heavy pace. The strong wind would throw off the course of an arrow, so he doubted the man would attempt such a feat. On a calm day without wind, he did not doubt the man could probably hit his mark, but under these circumstances that did not seem likely.

Tate also thought it possible that during the night the man might simply swim across and knife him in his sleep or split his skull with a war club. But for the past two nights the sky had been overcast making it almost impossible to see, so Tate was not concerned.

It was Tate's habit to rise each morning and make his way a few hundred yards to the north to a group of towering pines. What the Indian did not know is Tate habitually climbed the tallest one, from where he had a good view of the land around him. Three days ago he had spotted the lone Indian headed his way, riding a black and white paint pony. He had seen no other Indians, so he reasoned this Indian preferred to hunt by himself. Tate also knew he was at least a four-day ride from the nearest Blackfeet village, and so he did not consider this lone Indian to be much of a threat. A small war party might give him more concern, but he had a Spencer Carbine which held seven shots, and his pistol held six cartridges. He could stand off a half dozen raiders easily, especially where he was now situated.

The river in front of him had a fairly swift current, and although one might have a fair chance swimming to mid point, the current was hellishly strong in the center. He had tried to cross this area with his horses four weeks ago and finally had to cross several miles down and work his way up to this horseshoe bend where he was guarded from the north by the river on three sides. To the south, the distance between the severe bend of the river was no more than a couple hundred yards across and thick with trees and heavy undergrowth.

Because he was on the bend of the river did not mean he was cornered in case of an attack. When he first arrived, he had built a raft on which he could place at least his appaloosa riding horse and pole himself and the horse across in an emergency. If that happened, he would have to leave all his pelts behind along with his two packhorses, but saving his skin came first, and once he was astride his appaloosa, no Indian on any of their short legged ponies could catch him. None of this was new to Tate, since he had been chased out of Indian Territory before.

In the past three days, Tate had learned a lot about his Indian visitor. The man was cautious and careful, and had spent long hours observing him and his habits. On more than one occasion, Tate had seen the Indian sneak in to his secluded spot in the brush, and he had also seen him crawl back out. Sometimes the Indian would be gone for hours at a time, but he always seemed to return to the same spot, and always toward evening for sure. To throw the man off, Tate had sometimes spread his bedroll near his fire, and when it died out he moved his position. He also had got up in the middle of the night and moved his horses so that the Indian would not know their precise location.

During the day, Tate had checked his traps, because the Indian would expect him to do so, but he had cut his time short and periodically returned to his camp at various hours simply to confuse the observer. Sometimes he took a horse with him, sometimes he took all three as he moved about on this heavily wooded peninsula.

There was no doubt in Tate's mind, the Indian wanted his horses or at least one of them, otherwise he wouldn't have stuck around this long. Tate gave the man credit; he was cautious and cunning. Alone this far away from his tribe meant the warrior had to be extremely careful, since there was no one to back him up if the two ever got into a skirmish. Since the man did not leave to get other warriors, Tate assumed a little bit of greed was keeping the man here by himself. That was usually the case with a young Buck who wanted to make a name for himself in his village.

But Tate was not looking for a fight, and though he knew the man's exact position even now, he did not intend to kill the man. He was reasonably sure he could hit him with his rifle, but there was the off chance the bullet would strike one of the branches in front of the man and glance off.

Besides, what would that prove? Kill a man simply because he was doing a day's work, even though it might require stealing his horses?

Tate was not a killer. He was a trapper.

———— ♦ ————

When nightfall came Two Bears was still watching the camp across from him. He had eaten the last of his pemmican and dried elk meat, a six-day supply he had taken along since he left his camp. He had gone hungry for many days at a time before, so just because he was out of food did not necessarily mean he had to act tonight. But he was happy to see the clouds were dispersing. Periodic cloud cover along with a half moon would serve him well tonight.

At the moment he could still see the trapper, but the man was already moving his horses deeper into the foliage. Two Bears watched intently and counted slowly in his head to the number 150 until he saw the trapper emerge from the woods again. That meant if Two Bears walked in the same direction the trapper did and counted to 75, he should find the horses tethered together in an area no more than an arrow-shot distance from his camp. That was invaluable information.

Two Bears grinned, satisfied with his plan, satisfied that tonight he would be the owner of at least one of the man's horses.

He sat patiently through most of the night, and when the clouds broke, he left his bow and arrows and war club on shore along with his outer buckskin clothing. He silently slipped into the river wearing only his breechclout, the only weapon on him, his knife in a scabbard tied about his waist. He also carried several feet of braided rope coiled and draped over his head, something he would need to tether the horses together.

He slipped into the river and had made only a few strokes when he felt the swift current pushing him down stream. He moved fairly easily, but when he reached the middle of the river he began to dog paddle furiously. He had observed this river for the past three days and was suddenly in awe at how deceiving the strength of its flow was. But Two Bears was persistent, and because the river was slowly sweeping him further down stream, he was forced to swim even harder. Soon he was swimming overhand, something he did not want to do, but without the extra concerted effort, he would not get across.

When he first slipped into the river, he had judged the cloud cover well, hoping it would conceal him from view should the trapper be alert for any reason. But now, the cloud cover had disappeared, and he was sure he was visible in the moonlight. Yet, he kept swimming fiercely until he finally reached the opposite bank. When he pulled himself up on shore, he swore silently as he sat to catch his wind. He had drifted a considerable distance away from the white man's camp, and now he must make his way back through the thick trees and foliage, which would require a lot of precious time. He glanced upward calculating how long it would be before the sun would break the horizon. He was sure he had ample time to steal the horses, but he would have to be swift.

As he made his way through the brush, the mosquitoes swarmed on him and made his efforts all the more miserable, but Two Bears could not get the horses out of his head. No matter what the price, the animals would be worth it.

He moved steadily along the bank, careful not to make any sound, all the while cursing the error in judgement he had made concerning the strength of the river.

———— ♦ ————

Tate, after he had bedded down for the night, got up when the cloud cover darkened and made his way a few hundred yards to the north of his camp where he once again climbed the highest tree, from where he had a good command of the area around him.

If the Indian was going to make a move, it would be tonight, since the intermittent cloud cover would be in his favor. He did not expect the Indian to attempt the river before midnight, but just to be on the safe side, he decided to remain awake all night long. If he was wrong, he could still catch some sleep during the day.

But he was not wrong. Somewhere near three in the morning, he saw the movement in the stream far to the south. He knew the dark spot on the water was not a beaver, for he had trapped every one along that bank weeks ago. He kept his eye on the dark spot in the water, and when the spot reached near mid stream, he knew the Indian was making his attempt. He could easily see the current driving the man further down stream, and then he could see him as he stroked heavily to fight the center of the strong current. He could imagine the Indian by now must have been surprised at the force of the river, and he knew when the red man reached the other side, any bear grease he might have smeared on his face would be gone. Tate figured the Indian had more than likely shed his outer buckskin clothing and had crossed the river wearing only his breechclout. If that were the case, the mosquitoes would more than likely be making a meal out of him the rest of the morning,

A slight wind was blowing at him in the treetop, which was cooling and refreshing, and there were no mosquitoes at this height. From where Tate was perched, he could easily see his three horses corralled in an open space off to his left. Once the Indian reached his camp, he should know which direction Tate had taken his horses, and if the Indian was smart, he would have calculated earlier how far from camp he had moved them.

Moments ago Tate had seen the Indian reach the far bank and climb onto shore, but now he could not see him. Tate figured the Indian was making his way along the shore, careful of every step he made.

Tate sat patiently, still enjoying the cool breeze, knowing that in another fifteen or twenty minutes, the Indian was certain to locate his horses.

———— ◆ ————

Two Bears made his way through the trees, slowly, being careful not to give himself away by stepping on a rotten branch, or even tripping in the night. He did not know how much time had passed, but finally he could smell the smoke from the smoldering fire of the white man's camp. In the dim light, he could not see the trapper lying near the fire, but that did not surprise him. He had a good idea where the trapper's horses were located, and his only concern was that the white man might have moved his bedroll somewhere near them. Two Bears would have to tread lightly and hope he would not run across the man accidentally. If he did, he would have to kill him, which he did not want to do. But just in case he did...

———— ◆ ————

Tate's patience paid off. There was a period of time when he could clearly see his horses, but then the clouds darkened for an unusually long time, and when the cloud cover broke he saw that his three horses were gone. It was what Tate expected, and he also knew that no matter how hard the Indian tried, he would have a devil of a time getting all three horses across the river, unless he moved down river four or five miles. But that would throw off his timetable, so he would have to cross near here. Tate was convinced the Indian could get only one horse, and if this Indian was smart, he would take just the appaloosa and forget the other two.

The Indian was taking all three of his horses at the moment, and that was exactly what Tate expected him to do. So, quite calmly, he climbed down the tree, made his way to where he had his raft cached, and quickly poled himself across to the other side of the river.

———— ◆ ————

Two Bears was jubilant! He had managed to reach the horses and was now leading them away to the south away from the camp. Not once had he seen the trapper, and by the time the white man would rise in the morning, he would discover his horses were gone. By then, Two Bears would be well on his way back to his village.

Silently, yet quickly, Two Bears made his way through the trees for the longest time until he felt he was far enough away from the white man's camp. Along the way, mosquitoes continued to swarm about him, but he fought them off, all the while gloating in his prize catch.

He knew it would be a difficult task getting three horses across the river, but these were great animals, worthy of much praise. On the bank, he carefully tethered the tail of the appaloosa to a make-shift bridle on one of the sorrels and did the same from the second to the third horse. He then led the appaloosa into the water, and with a firm grip on his mane, he urged him forward. The other's fell in behind, but once in the water, the current caught them, and the appaloosa faltered, fighting the weight of the horses pulling at him.

The appaloosa turned and drifted with the current, and soon he was headed back to shore, the other two in tow. Two Bears cursed, trying desperately to keep the head of the appaloosa pointed toward the opposite bank. It was all Two Bears could do to keep himself afloat, and trying to keep the horses heading across in addition taxed his strength and became a most formidable task.

Back on the shoreline, Two Bears was exhausted, but determined. He caught his breath and headed the horses into the water again, and after only a minute or so, the current again forced them back to shore.

Two Bears grunted, crawled on shore all out of breath, his strength almost all gone. He rested for a long time and calmed the horses, talking to them, petting them alongside their necks, encouraging them. All the while he was chanting to the Great Spirit in hopes the Great One would give him the strength to bring these wonderful horses to the other side.

And so Two Bears, now angry and frustrated and chewed up by a thousand mosquitoes, tried again and again and again.

———— ◆ ————

Tate had easily poled himself across the river, and with his rifle in hand he made his way through the trees, all of this area quite familiar to him. It did not take him long to locate the Indian's paint, since he knew precisely where the Indian had tied him to a tree. Tate discovered the horse while it was still dark, and after having waited an hour in a secluded area, he was mildly surprised that the Indian had not yet returned. When the sun broke the horizon and the Indian had still not appeared to pick up his paint, Tate began to think he misjudged him. Yet, he could not conceive that any Indian would leave his horse behind under any circumstances. This paint, though a small horse, was sure to be the Indian's most prized horse. A Blackfoot would not journey four days from his camp on a nag, so Tate reasoned the man would return for his horse, and he was counting heavily on such logic.

But now, a half-hour after the sun was up, the Indian had still not returned, and Tate was no longer sure he had calculated the Indian's moves correctly.

He had taken the paint fifty yards up on a rise to a point where he had a good view of the surrounding area, and he was carefully hidden in a group of aspens.

His concerns promptly disappeared when he heard the sound of hoof beats off to his right. A deer trail meandered along this side of the river, and it was here that Tate was sure the Indian would appear riding his appaloosa.

And suddenly there he was. The Indian was coming up the trail astride his appaloosa, and behind him were his two packhorses! Tate gaped, astounded that the Indian, a small man in stature, had managed to get all three horses across the swift current of the river.

Through the trees, Tate watched as the Indian brought the appaloosa to a halt and looked around. He was searching for his paint, and by the look on his face, he was more than puzzled why his horse was missing.

It was then Tate nudged the paint beneath him into the open. He was on the hill above the Indian, the rifle draped across his lap. Two Bears turned and suddenly saw the trapper astride his own horse. He also saw the rifle in the white man's hand, but he was relieved to see that the white man did not have it pointed at him.

Though Two Bears had donned his buckskin clothes and now had the bow and quiver draped over his head, he knew he could not remotely get an arrow off before the white man could shoot him. Yet the white man did not make any threatening gesture. He simply sat still, sitting tall on his prized paint. When the white man urged the paint on and slowly started walking down the hill, Two Bears stiffened and could feel the sweat cover his forehead. Only feet away, the white man stopped. Two Bears stared for the longest time at the trapper. Never had he seen a white man from this close before. He was surprised that the man's skin wasn't as white as he thought it should be. In fact, the man's face and hands were tanned heavily, like his own skin.

Slowly Tate slipped off the paint to the ground, then walked forward and held out the reins toward the Indian. Two Bears understood immediately. He slid off the appaloosa and offered the reins of the three stolen horses across to the white man, and in seconds the trade was made.

It was clear to Two Bears that he was getting his horse back, and more importantly, he had also been granted his life, for surely this white man could easily have shot him dead. Two Bears suddenly had the highest admiration for this white man. The trapper had known precisely what Two Bears had intended to do, and he had calculated carefully and outsmarted him at every turn. This, for Two Bears, had been a hard lesson, but it was one he would cherish forever.

With a swift move, Two Bears mounted his horse, and in sign language he thanked the white man for granting him his life. Tate, no stranger to the language of the plains, signed back that today the Great Spirit had watched over both of them.

Two Bears knew he had met a man of honor, and for that he was very grateful. He rode up the rise, and when he turned he saw the trapper had mounted his horse and was headed back toward the river, his two packhorses behind him.

Two Bears was a proud man, and although the past few days had not gone in his favor, he would tell this event to his newly acquired wife when he returned to camp. He would also tell this story to his children if the Great Spirit would grant him some, and he would relate this as well to all of his grandchildren if he lived long enough.

For this was the day that made Two Bears a humble man.

To order additional copies of
A Time For Justice And Other Frontier Tales
please complete the following.

$16.95 each *(plus $3.50 shipping & handling)*

Please send me _____ additional books at $ _____ each

Shipping and Handling costs for larger quantites available upon request.

Bill my: ❑ VISA ❑ MasterCard Expires _____

Card # _____

Signature _____

Daytime Phone Number _____

For credit card orders call 1-888-568-6329

OR SEND THIS ORDER FORM TO:
McCleery & Sons Publishing
PO Box 248
Gwinner, ND 58040-0248

I am enclosing $_____
❑ Check ❑ Money Order

Payable in US funds. No cash accepted.

SHIP TO:

Name_____

Mailing Address _____

City _____

State/Zip _____

Orders by check allow longer delivery time.
Money order and credit card orders will be shipped within 48 hours.
This offer is subject to change without notice.

Also by Kent Kamron:

Charlie's Gold and Other Frontier Tales
Kamron's first collection of short stories. In the same vein as *A Time for Justice*, this collection of thirteen short stories (174 pages) gives you adventure tales about men and women of the west, made up of cowboys, Indians, settlers, gunslingers and other colorful characters. $15.95 in paper back. (plus $2.50 shipping & handling)

A Time for Cowboys
Coming in December or early spring, 2001.
Kamron's novel, set in 1869, traces the bold adventures of a young cowboy, Carter Cole. Set on building a cattle ranch, he sets off into Indian Territory in search of maverick cattle. He joins two desperadoes being pursued by a posse, but this along with gunfights, hangings, rustlers and Indians does not hamper his determination to gather up a herd. Approximately 350 pages.

Pete's New Family

Pete's New Family is a groundbreaking book for children and caring parents who are experiencing divorce. Hailed by professionals in preschool and child development counseling, this "kinder, gentler" story is a helpful aid for parents who put kids first, even when marriage fails. Most important, Pete's New Family is a tale for children (ages 4-8) lovingly written to help youngsters understand events that they are powerless to change. Written by a single mom and Head Start volunteer, Pete's New Family is an unabashed endorsement of considerate, constructive behavior in the warring arena of divorce.

Sought after by counselors, pastors and teachers, Pete's New Family is available at special book rates for counseling professionals, schools and libraries.
Written by Brenda Jacobson
$9.95 each (plus $2.50 each shipping & handling) (price breaks after qty. of 10)

Bonanza Belle

In 1908, Carrie Amundson left her home and family in Spring Grove, MN, to follow her brother to North Dakota, where they both become employed on a bonanza farm. After several years toiling in the bonanza farm's kitchen, Carrie married and moved to town. One tragedy after the other befell her and altered her life considerably. Eventually she found herself back on the farm, where her new family lived and toiled during the Great Depression. Carrie changed from a carefree young girl to a grown woman of great depth and stamina. Her strong faith in God was evident in the way she reacted to happenings outside her control and how she lived each day of her life.
Written by Elaine Ulness Swenson. (344 pgs.)
$12.50 each (plus $2.50 ea. shipping & handling)

First The Dream

As a young child in Norway, Anna Olsen begins dreaming about leaving the beautiful but confining hills that surround her family's farm in the scenic Hailing valley of Norway. As a young woman she becomes a teacher but never forgets her dream. After an unwanted marriage proposal, she makes the decision to leave her homeland. In 1905, at age 19, Anna arrives in America to join three of her siblings who came ten years earlier. This story spans ninety years of a woman's life. Anna finds love, loses it, and finds it once again. A secret that Anna has kept since her first year in this country, is fully revealed only at the end of her life.
Written by Elaine Ulness Swenson. (326 pgs.)
$12.50 each (plus $2.50 ea. shipping & handling)

Charlies Gold and Other Frontier Tales
Written by Kent Kamron. (174 pgs.)
$15.95 each (plus $2.50 shipping & handling)